Milton Hershey

Illustrated by
Meryl Henderson

Milton Hershey

YOUNG CHOCOLATIER

by M.M. Eboch

ALADDIN PAPERBACKS
New York   London   Toronto   Sydney

This book is a work of fiction. Any references to historical events,
real people, or real locales are used fictitiously. Other names,
characters, places, and incidents are the product of the author's
imagination, and any resemblance to actual events or locales or
persons, living or dead, is entirely coincidental.

ALADDIN PAPERBACKS
An imprint of Simon & Schuster Children's Publishing Division
1230 Avenue of the Americas, New York, NY 10020
Text copyright © 2008 by M.M. Eboch
Illustrations copyright © 2008 by Meryl Henderson
All rights reserved, including the right of reproduction
in whole or in part in any form.
ALADDIN PAPERBACKS, CHILDHOOD OF
FAMOUS AMERICANS, and related logo are
registered trademarks of Simon & Schuster, Inc.
Designed by Lisa Vega
The text of this book was set in New Caledonia.
Manufactured in the United States of America
First Aladdin Paperbacks edition July 2008
2 4 6 8 10 9 7 5 3 1
Library of Congress Control Number 2007934394
ISBN-13: 978-1-4169-5569-6
ISBN-10: 1-4169-5569-0

ILLUSTRATIONS

CONTENTS

Oil Town

"Look over there, Milton," Henry Hershey said.

Milton looked where his father pointed. A railroad car was parked along the street, like a house on wheels.

"Fortunes are made in there," his father said. "Men who know how to dream big and take chances become millionaires overnight." He looked down at his son and grinned. "Like you and me, right? Someday we'll be living in a mansion and have the best of everything.

No more brown bread for breakfast and cabbage stew for supper. We'll drive a carriage and go out to the theater."

Reports of the first oil wells had hit the newspapers a year earlier, in 1860. Thousands of men had rushed to the Pennsylvania oil fields. These men still crowded the streets, dressed in rough work clothes. They drank in the saloons and fought in the streets.

But Milton's father, Henry, was different. He wore a silk suit and carried a gold-tipped walking stick. He spoke well, laughed often, and told wonderful stories. Milton took his father's hand, and his heart swelled with pride.

Milton and his father picked their way carefully through the muddy streets of Titusville. A sheen of oil glistened in the puddles. The air reeked of rotting food and outhouses. It almost covered up the bitter smell of crude oil from the oil wells all around town. When they passed a dead mule, the stench rose up so strong that Milton's eyes stung. He covered his nose and mouth with his hands.

They turned into a twisting alley at the edge of town. When they rounded a corner near the shack where they lived, Milton's eyes almost popped out of his head. A wagon stood outside their open door. Two men were loading luggage into it.

Milton's father paused for a moment, then strode forward. "Abraham! Benjamin! Wonderful to see you."

The men frowned at him. Henry lifted Milton into the wagon. "Milton, my boy, these are your uncles Abraham and Benjamin Snavely. You haven't seen them in more than a year, but you've heard your mother talk about her brothers."

The men nodded to Milton. They were dressed alike, in plain, dark suits. They had short, graying beards. Henry Hershey, tall and lean, towered over them. His luxurious black beard stood out in contrast to theirs.

"Have you come to invest more money in the oil boom?" Milton's father asked.

"We came to check on our sister," Abraham said. "And now we're going to take her home."

Milton's mother stepped out of the shack. She stood between her brothers, a short, round-shouldered woman. A simple gray dress hung over her pregnant stomach. Lines etched the face under her bonnet.

"This is no place for women and children," Abraham said. "Gunfights, murders in the streets, fires, explosions, and all this filth!"

"Fanny is used to better," Benjamin said softly. He gestured to Milton. "How old is he, four and a half? He is as puny as a three-year-old. Get him back to the farm, where he can have fresh milk and eggs every day."

Fanny Hershey's thin lips turned up in a smile. "Yes," she breathed.

"But you don't understand!" Henry cried. "With this war, the Union army needs oil.

Men are becoming millionaires and helping a good cause at the same time. Fortune is just around the corner."

"That's what you said fifteen months ago," Abraham said.

"But this time it's different!" Henry insisted. "Oil runs into low land, and I know a prospector who will sell a share of his claim. He needs the money to keep digging."

Abraham frowned. "And six months ago you said you would find oil close to the creek. What happened to the money we gave you then?"

"I just need a little more," Henry pleaded. "Please. It's for Fanny and Milton, and the baby."

"We have money to help them," Benjamin said. "And we'll use it to move all of you back home."

Henry turned to Milton's mother. "Fanny, you don't want to give up now. Just think of all we could have when I find oil."

She shook her head. "I'm sorry, but I can't

live like this anymore. I can't bring up my children here!"

"But it's for them! Our future!"

"You've had your chance. You have to give up this dream." She turned back to the shack. Henry followed her, still pleading.

Milton sat on the wagon, trying to make sense of it all.

"That man," Benjamin said. "He would feed wheat to his cow, to get sweeter cream for his porridge. Only the good Lord knows why she ever married him."

"I don't think the good Lord had anything to do with it," Abraham said. "Henry walked away from the faith years ago. He tricked Fanny with his fancy promises in order to get at our money."

Benjamin sighed. "But do you remember how lively she used to be? She was a dreamer too."

"Not anymore," Abraham said. "This adventure has taught her a lesson. Perhaps next time she'll listen to her family."

Benjamin glanced at Milton. "It is too late to turn back the clock. But we can make sure this little fellow has a decent start in life."

Milton looked away. He knew his parents fought, but he loved them both. His mother was stern but stable, a comforting rock. His father was fun and adventurous. Why couldn't they be happy together?

Soon they had the wagon loaded. Milton sat up front between his mother and Uncle Abraham. His father sat in the back, dangling his long legs over the edge and gazing back at the oil fields.

As they left Titusville, the hillsides were covered with nothing but tree stumps. The oil had turned the creek purple and blue. Snow dusted the ground, but it had already turned gray from the grime. Bright pennants hanging from oil derricks added little color to the dull scene.

They passed a wagon filled with huge barrels of oil. Tired mules struggled to pull it along the muddy road. A distant boom of dynamite rattled the wagon, and the horses danced nervously. Milton snuggled closer to his mother, who wrapped her cloak warmly around him. Eventually, the swaying of the wagon and clopping of the horses' hooves lulled him to sleep.

They stayed the night in Oil City, twenty miles from Titusville. In the morning they boarded a riverboat. As the boat drew farther from the oil fields, Milton sniffed the air. It smelled different to him somehow. He turned to his mother. "What's that smell?"

She gave a coarse laugh. "That is fresh air, son. No more stink of oil like a fog over the town."

Milton gazed in wonder as they floated past snow-covered farm fields. His mother and father told him that he had been born on a farm, but he didn't remember anything about those first years. They had moved to Titusville just before his third birthday. All he knew was the tiny shack, the muddy town streets, and the smell of oil and garbage.

They switched to a larger boat, and went on to Pittsburgh. From there they traveled by rail toward Lancaster, Pennsylvania. Milton's mother talked quietly with her brothers about farming, family, and their Mennonite religion.

Milton watched the changing scenery and studied the wonderful ferryboat and train. For him, the best part of the trip was the food. He had plenty to eat, including luxuries such as meat. He knew his father was upset, and Milton felt bad about that. But he found himself looking forward to the future, full of clean air and good food, like his uncles promised.

His uncle Benjamin even bought him a bag of chewy caramels. The sweet flavor washed over Milton's tongue. He had never tasted anything so wonderful! He looked across the aisle to where his father sat staring out of the window. Henry Hershey had stopped trying to change the Snavely minds once they left Oil City. He hadn't said much all day.

Milton tottered across the aisle and held out his sticky bag of caramels. "Do you want one, Papa? They are good." Maybe the sweets would make him feel better too.

Henry smiled down at his son. "Thank you, my boy." He took one and chewed it slowly. "Delicious."

Milton climbed up on the seat next to his father. He glanced at his uncles. "Do we have to live with those men now?" he whispered.

Henry grinned at him. "No, my boy, we'll go back to the Hershey homestead. Then we'll move on to our next adventure."

Milton's eyes shone. "What will that be?"

His father gazed dreamily out the window. "I've always wanted to be a writer. How would you like a famous author for a father, my boy?"

Treats and Threats

"Oh, there you are, Milton. Did you finish your chores?"

"Yes, Mother. I fed the chickens, and here are the eggs."

She took the basket from him. "Good boy. We will leave in a few minutes."

Milton ran into the next room, where his baby sister played. He bent down and gave her a hug. "Sarena, it's market day. We get to ride the wagon into town!" She giggled and smiled at him. He leaned closer and whispered, "Maybe Papa will give me a penny for candy. I'll share with you if he does."

They loaded the farm wagon with the brooms Fanny Hershey had made, the butter she had churned that week, and some extra eggs. Milton lifted Sarena up to their mother and climbed in after her. Henry flicked the reins to get the old horse moving, and they started for Harrisburg.

Henry told them a story called "The Three Little Pigs" and then began to sing a funny song: "Away down South in the land of traitors/Rattlesnakes and alligators/ Right away, come away, right away, come away!"

"Why must you expose the children to such frivolous and ungodly nonsense?" Fanny snapped. She followed the ways of the Reformed Mennonite Church, and they believed that entertainment like county fairs and horse races, and even foolish talking, were carnal sins.

Henry had long since walked away from the Mennonite faith. He gave an airy wave of his hand. "I have no use for you gray-minded people who cannot rejoice."

Fanny spent the rest of the ride in stony silence. Milton did not like seeing his mother unhappy, but he had to giggle at his father's funny tale about a little man named Rumpelstiltskin. He could not understand why the newspapers would not buy the stories his father wrote. Milton thought he had the funniest father in the world.

At last they reached Harrisburg, the capital city of Pennsylvania. The Hersheys rode down a street past fine mansions, all several stories high.

They set up in the market. Milton watched Sarena as his parents sold their goods. When the bustle died down, Fanny took the sleeping child from Milton's arms.

Henry held out his hand to Milton. "Come, my boy. Let's see the sights."

Fanny frowned. "Don't you be spending the money we just made. Pennies saved grow into dollars."

Henry merely tipped his hat to her and started down the street. They passed a bank and a large hotel. Henry and Milton paused to look through the windows of a general store and a bakery.

Then they came to the confectionery shop. Milton's eyes widened as he gazed through the glass. Shop boys in white aprons served well-dressed customers. Young couples laughed over their sweets. Milton's mouth watered.

"What do you think, my boy?" his father asked. "Shall we take some refreshment in this fine establishment?"

Milton looked up at his father. "Oh, yes, Papa, only . . ." He trailed off, remembering his mother's words.

Henry smiled at him and pulled a shiny penny from his pocket. It glittered in the sunlight, and Milton grinned. "What is the value

of life, without the little joys?" Henry asked. They went into the shop and ate their fill of ice cream and lemon pastry.

Milton watched the shop boys as he ate. How wonderful to work in a place like this! You could eat ice cream and candy all day long. As they were leaving he said, "Oh! Sarena! I promised I would share with her if I got some candy."

His father nodded solemnly. "Of course, we must not forget little Sarena." He turned back and bought a bag of lemon drops. He tucked the bag into Milton's pocket. "Save these for later, though," he said with a wink, "and don't tell your mother."

Milton made the lemon drops last by taking only one piece each day for himself, and giving one to Sarena. Since she was just over a year old, he had to watch her carefully while she sucked the treat. The candy was a reminder of the wonders of the city. There, the boys wore white aprons and served ice cream, instead of carrying water, feeding chickens, and gathering eggs every day.

Eventually, the candy ran out, and Milton could only look forward to the next trip. But his parents were not talking about market day. Henry Hershey got the *New York Times* and a local paper, the *Lancaster Inquirer*. In late June of 1863, the papers were filled with news of the Civil War between the North and South.

"The Confederate army is moving toward Pennsylvania under Robert E. Lee," Henry said as his eyes scanned the paper one night.

Members of the Reformed Mennonite Church did not even believe in voting. "Why do you insist on reading that thing?" Fanny sniffed. "It is a waste of money."

"You can't always hide from what is going on in the world," Henry said.

Fanny laughed. "You think I don't know? After we left that miserable oil town, you said my brothers kept you from getting rich. But oil prices crashed last year when fools dug too many wells. You didn't pass along that news, but I heard it. And now I do all the work while you keep scheming and dreaming."

"There was a time when you dreamed too."

"Yes," Fanny said. "Before I learned that dreaming is all you do. Prosperity comes from hard work, not chasing dreams."

Henry frowned and flipped the newspaper up in front of his face. "Listen to this. It says, 'The danger to Pennsylvania and the North is still imminent. Everything depends upon the encounter between Lee and General Meade. If our army should be defeated we should have no hope, except in large armies to be raised in the North.'"

Milton slid out of his chair and stood next to his father. "What does that mean, Papa?"

Henry set down the paper and put a hand on Milton's shoulder. "A great battle is brewing.

19

You know that we are at war, to force the Southern states to free the slaves. It is an honorable cause. Now the Southern army is moving north, and our own Union troops are going to meet them. The earth will tremble when those great armies clash! And it may very well be here on our own doorstep."

"You're scaring the child," Fanny said.

"He will be a man soon, and he should know what is happening in the world," Henry said. "It is his future too."

Milton looked anxiously toward the front door. "But what can we do?"

Henry stroked his beard. "Some families are fleeing to the North."

"We cannot leave the farm," Fanny said. "I will not let those savage soldiers destroy my garden."

"Some people are burying their money," Henry went on. "That way, if Southern soldiers take over, they will not be able to steal."

Fanny stood up with a swish of skirts. "We

do not have that worry, anyway. We have no valuables." She strode from the room.

Milton thought of the few coins he owned, hidden in a handkerchief in his room. He did not want anything to happen to them. He went to the front window and looked out, scanning the dusk for any sign of soldiers. "Papa! What is that strange light?"

Henry joined Milton by the window. They gazed out at a distant glow along the horizon. The orange light seemed to ooze into the sky. "That must be the battle," Henry said. "Something is on fire. I hope our brave boys are all right." Milton shivered, and Henry's hand tightened on his shoulder. They watched in silence until Milton could not keep his eyes open any longer. Henry carried him to bed.

The Sounds of War

When Milton woke in the morning, he dressed quickly and looked for his father. Henry was not in the house, the barn, or the yard. Milton found his mother on the porch. The butter churn spun in her hands. Sarena played with a rag doll nearby. "Mother," Milton said, "where is Papa?"

"Who knows what that man is up to now," Fanny grumbled.

"But, Mother—"

"Get to your chores," Fanny said.

Milton headed for the chicken coop. Where could Papa be? A chill ran over him. What if the soldiers had gotten his father! Milton paused outside the chicken coop. Southern soldiers might be hiding inside.

Milton looked back at his mother. With Papa gone, he was the man of the house. He had to be brave. He took a deep breath and stuck his head into the coop. His heart pounded as he peered around in the dim light.

A chicken squawked, and Milton jumped. He took another deep breath. His nose filled with the stench of chickens and their droppings. Milton laughed. *Nobody would want to spend the night in here*, he thought.

He fed the chickens and gathered their eggs. He carried water from the pump to the house and brought firewood in for the stove. Finally, he fed Sarena and rocked her to sleep in her crib on the porch.

At last he heard the clop of horse's hooves and saw dust rising from the road. He squinted until he could make out the form. "Papa!" Milton raced forward. He held the reins while his father climbed down. "Where did you go?" Milton demanded.

Henry held up a folded newspaper. "I didn't want to wait for this. Big things are happening, and we should know about them. Let's take care of the horse, and then I'll tell you all about it."

A few minutes later, the horse was grazing in the field. Milton sat with his father at the kitchen table. Henry opened the newspaper and spread it out. "Yesterday, the Southern army took over the city of York. That's only twenty-five miles from here. The people simply turned over their city, without a fight. Not a shot fired!" Henry shook his head in disapproval. "That's what comes from this pacifist stance. It's easy to say that war is wrong, but sometimes you have to fight, to protect what you love."

He kept reading. "Last night, the Union army set fire to the covered bridge over the

Susquehanna River. That bridge is a mile long, and it burned all night. That's the glow we saw in the sky last night."

He folded up the newspaper and gazed at Milton. "We must be ready for anything, my boy."

Milton nodded. But what could he do? He went to his room and unwrapped the handkerchief with his few coins. He had to protect them from the soldiers. If people buried their valuables, that's what he would do.

He found an old coffee can and tucked his coins inside it. Then he slipped out to the garden. He gazed in every direction. He had to make sure no enemy soldier was hiding and watching him. Nothing stirred in the hot, still air.

Milton took a spade and quickly dug a hole. He pushed the coffee can inside it and covered it with dirt. He stepped back to look at his work. The dirt looked different from the area around it; he had patted it down too firmly. Milton went back to work, spreading

the dirt in soft clumps so it all looked the same. Finally satisfied, he glanced around again and scurried back to the house. No Southern soldier would get his coins now!

Two days later, on July 1, Milton woke up to a distant rumble just after dawn. He leaped from bed and rushed to a window. Clouds turned the sky gray. Nothing moved outside but a squirrel and some birds.

Milton dressed and went into the kitchen. His father was standing in the doorway, gazing out. He turned to his son and said, "The battle has begun."

Milton shivered. His mother did not say anything, but she gave him a quick hug.

All morning the rumble of distant cannons continued. If he put his ear to the ground, Milton could even hear a sharp noise, like guns going off. He wondered about the men who were fighting. Some of them might die. War was a terrible thing.

In his community, few people had joined the army. Most Mennonites were abolitionists, who thought slavery should end. But they did not believe in fighting. Milton wished the country did not have to go to war. Why couldn't people treat one another with kindness?

All that day, people passed by in horse-drawn wagons piled high with furniture. A few stopped to call out to Milton's father. "Hershey! You'd best get out. Lee has crossed the Susquehanna and he's heading for Philadelphia!"

"We'll wait a little longer," Henry Hershey said.

"But, Papa," Milton said, "what if the soldiers come?"

"I have faith in our boys," Henry said. He glanced back at the house and chuckled. "Besides, your mother would insist upon taking the chickens. I won't share the wagon with those nasty birds."

Milton stayed close to the house all day. He wanted to keep an eye on his mother and Sarena. He went from window to window, gazing out over the fields. Maybe he would be the first to see the Southern soldiers approach. He could give the alarm and be a hero!

But then they would have to flee, and that would be awful. Maybe they would wind up someplace like Titusville. He knew his father missed the excitement of the oil camp, but Milton thought the farm was nicer. The chickens smelled bad, but nowhere near as bad as the oil wells. He and Sarena could play outside. They had plenty to eat, and milk every day. If they wanted water, they got it from the pump. In Titusville, even drinking water cost money.

Milton gazed around at the little farm, and tears sprang to his eyes. He loved this quiet valley with its farm fields and dairy cows. This had to be the best place in the whole world. He hoped it would never change.

• • •

Though the cannon rumble continued for days, Milton never saw a soldier. The rumor that Lee has crossed the Susquehanna was false. The Northern army had won at Gettysburg. Within a week, the families that had fled were coming home again.

"It's all over now," his father said after reading the paper one day. "The South doesn't have a chance." His usual smile faded. "Who would have thought this war could last so long, or cost so much? Thousands died at Gettysburg, on both sides." He sighed. "We can only hope our country never sees a war like this again."

Milton didn't know what to say. He found Sarena and gave her a hug. "You're too young to understand about war," he whispered. "You're lucky. I hope we never have another one. But if we do, don't worry. I'll protect you."

He went out to the garden to dig up his coffee can full of coins. He stopped and stared at the rows of vegetables. "It was between the corn and beans. . . . No, it was by the tomatoes. . . ." He frowned and looked around. Where did he bury the can? It all looked the same!

Milton tried digging in one spot, and then another. By the end of the day, he had dozens of holes all over the garden but he still hadn't found his coins.

Finally his mother came out. "What on earth are you doing?"

Milton fought back tears. "I buried my money and now I can't find it!"

His mother stared at him, and then laughed. "You grow money by saving it, not by planting it!"

Eventually, Milton gave up. His coins were lost for good.

Big Dreams

Though the war ended, life did not get much better for the Hersheys. Henry tried to sell farm machinery, but failed. When they ran out of money and lost the Hershey homestead, Fanny's family gave them a small farm. Their new house was a small, drafty cabin. Still, it was miles away from Fanny's stern brothers. That made Henry happy, and he was full of big ideas.

One morning Henry sat at the table looking at some drawings. "I tell you, Fanny, this perpetual-motion machine will be a great success! Mr. Wohlgast is a genius. His machine is powered by a wheel, with weights that slide on rods. It will keep spinning forever!"

Fanny turned from the sink with her hands on her hips. "And what is the use of a machine like that?"

Henry gaped at her. "Men have been looking for a self-renewing source of energy for centuries! I tell you, with this invention, Wohlgast and Hershey will be on the tongues of all civilized men."

"They will be talked about as fools," Fanny snapped. "For once in your life, won't you settle down to work? You are almost forty!"

"I tell you, it is an excellent idea," Henry said as Milton peered down at the drawings. "If you will just tell Abraham and Benjamin—"

"I will not embarrass myself over your silly ideas. Look where they have gotten us so far. Most of our neighbors are getting wood-burning stoves, while I must do all my cooking on this kitchen hearth."

"You can thank your brothers for this house and this hearth," Henry said.

Milton looked away. He hated hearing his parents argue. Sarena, almost four years old, put down her doll and pulled on Fanny's skirt. "Don't be angry, Mama."

Fanny wiped her wet hands on her apron and bent to hug Sarena. "Do not worry, darling. Everything is fine." She stood up. "I need to finish washing these dishes. You be a good girl and play quietly."

"Come here and sit on my lap," Henry said. Sarena did, and giggled as her father tickled her.

Fanny handed Milton a warm muffin. "Go get some cherries from Mrs. Salisbury. Wait, take these to her." She gave him a basket and pushed him toward the door.

Milton stood on the porch to finish his muffin. He could still hear his parents arguing inside. It seemed as though they were always arguing about something. As Milton grew older, he understood that people saw his father as lazy. But Milton couldn't share his mother's anger. His father's stories and laughter did more to fill the long nights with warmth than money could.

Milton brushed the crumbs from his jacket and ran toward the ramshackle cherry farm where the African American widow lived.

"Good morning, Mrs. Salisbury," he called as he neared the farmhouse.

The elderly woman squinted from her rocking chair on the porch. She raised a hand in a wave as he got closer. "Good morning, child. What's that you have?"

Milton held out the basket he carried. "I came to get some cherries so Mother and Aunt Mattie can make a pie. Mother sent some eggs and butter in trade."

Mary Salisbury slowly rose to her feet. "She's a hard worker, your mother. How are you all enjoying life here?"

"I like it, and so does Sarena. Papa has big

plans. He even has a new name for our farm. Something fancy, but I forget exactly."

"And your mama? Has she settled in all right?"

Milton looked away. "She calls it the little stony farm."

Mary Salisbury chuckled. "She is right, at that. One has to wonder why your uncles set you up in that place."

"Papa likes it, though," Milton insisted. "He doesn't mind that the ground isn't so good. We're building a dam today and putting in a trout pond. Papa invited the neighbors to a party. He calls it a . . . a frolic, and they're all going to help."

She smiled. "Your father is a big dreamer."

Milton looked down at his feet and whispered, "Mother says his dreams are a waste of time."

Mary Salisbury reached out a bony hand and clasped his shoulder. "That's because she's given up on her own dreams. Your father never will. But I admit, it's hard for a woman to put up with a husband who doesn't feed and clothe his children properly."

Milton followed her gaze down to his bare feet. He had shoes, but he had grown so much that they pinched, so he only wore them to church. His tunic and knickers were worn and too small. Still, his mother always made sure his clothes were clean and well mended.

Mrs. Salisbury released his shoulder. She plucked a cherry from the bowl on the porch next to her. "A dream is like this cherry. It's pretty and sweet, but it doesn't last long." She worked her thumbs around the stem and pulled the cherry in two, until the pit showed. "But if you plant the seed, and give it water, and fertilizer, and everything else it needs, someday you can have a whole tree full of cherries. Dreams are like that too. They need hard work to make them come true."

Milton frowned, trying to make sense of everything she said.

"Did you know this house used to be a

stop on the Underground Railroad?" Mrs. Salisbury asked.

Milton nodded, and his eyes shone. "I've heard lots of stories about how people helped the runaway slaves."

"The people around here are good," Mrs. Salisbury said. "I couldn't survive here by myself, without my neighbors' help. But it takes more than just a good heart to make a difference. The people who started the Underground Railroad had big dreams. They worked for those dreams, fought for them, sometimes even died for them. The hard work was important. But it all started with a dream."

The Frolic

Back home, Milton went straight to the kitchen. His mother and her sister were inside, dressed alike in dark dresses and white bonnets.

"Good morning, Aunt Mattie," he said as she turned from the ice chest.

His mother's sister smiled at him. "There's my little man. Working hard, I see." She bent over, and he stretched up to give her a kiss on the cheek. She fished around in her apron pocket and pulled out a penny. "Here's something to add to your collection. Take good care of it."

"Thank you, Aunt Mattie!" Milton exchanged the basket of cherries for the penny.

As he went to put the coin away, he heard his mother say, "You are too generous."

"Nonsense," Aunt Mattie said. "He must learn how to handle money, and he won't get that from his father." Milton knew his aunt didn't like his father much. He had heard stories about how Henry Hershey had courted Mattie once, before Fanny. Mattie had never married, but she didn't seem to care. She spent more and more time at the Hershey household. Together Mattie and Fanny cooked, cleaned, cared for the children, and complained about Henry.

Milton hid his penny in a handkerchief. Then he slipped outside to watch the frolic. Some of the men had taken off their coats and rolled up their shirtsleeves. Henry Hershey wore his silk suit and top hat.

Milton was amazed to see how far the stone dam had already grown. Even some of his mother's relatives had come out to help. Milton had two cousins about his age, boys named Stoner and Rohrer. They worked slowly and carefully, seldom speaking and never smiling.

Milton slipped in next to them and started working. At eight years old, he couldn't carry the heavy stones, but he could steady them in place while a man slapped on masonry to hold them.

"What are you planning to call this place again?" the miller called.

"The Trout Brook Fruit and Nursery Farm," Henry Hershey answered. "I'll fill the pond with trout and goldfish. I'm also planting berry bushes, fruit trees and shrubs, new types to sell to farmers and home owners." He stepped back for a moment and stroked his beard. "I may sink a shaft in that northern field, as well. I have a feeling I might find ore there."

The men laughed. "You'll find dirt if you're lucky, and stones if you're not," a neighboring farmer teased.

Soon the talk turned to Lancaster, the nearest big city. "Has anyone been to the Fulton Theater lately?" Henry asked. "I hear they have an opera company from Philadelphia."

"That's too fancy for me," the miller said, "but I saw Commodore Foote, the smallest man in the world! He and his sister—she's tiny too—do dances and tell funny stories."

A teenager broke in. "If you want real entertainment, watch one of John Wise's balloon flights. He takes off from Centre Square, right among the buildings. Sometimes he can hardly get clear! When I saw him, a fellow had to lean out a window and push the balloon away to keep it from crashing into the wall."

"How can you waste time on such things, with so much suffering in the land?" asked a heavyset African American man in a dark coat and white collar.

"This isn't a sermon, Reverend." One of the farmers laughed. "Now put your shoulders into it and heave some rock!"

In a few hours, the men had completed their work. Henry stood back and gazed on the dam with a smile. "As soon as the rains swell the brook, we'll have a fine trout pond."

The men headed toward the house, pulling on their jackets. Neighbor women clustered on the lawn. A long table held the platters of food they had brought. Except on trips to the city, Milton had never seen so many women in bright clothes, or heard so much laughter. They wore dresses in plaid or prints, with full skirts, long sleeves, and high necklines. Sarena played with two other girls her age. Her own dark clothing looked drab next to the other girls' dresses. One wore orange and white checks, and the other had a dark pink dress.

Fanny and Aunt Mattie brought out their cherry pies, and everyone sat. After a prayer, they dug into the food. Chicken corn soup, stewed rabbit, corn bread, pickled eggs, sauerkraut, mushroom and tomato catsups, and more. For dessert they had several cakes, cobblers, and pies to choose from. Milton felt proud that the cherry pies were the best dessert of all.

Finally the women started cleaning up, while the men sat chatting. Sarena and the other girls ran away to play. Milton listened to the conversation for a few minutes, but they were talking about politics. He turned to his cousins, Stoner and Rohrer. "Do you want to play a game? We could play I Spy, or Hop, Step, and Jump."

They gazed at him with faces as serious as Abraham's and Benjamin's. "Frivolous activity is sinful," Stoner said.

Milton sighed and looked around for the girls. Maybe they would play a game with him. He spotted a flash of pink down by the dam and started toward it.

A scream pierced the air. Milton started running before the sound faded. He knew it had come from Sarena.

He reached the dam and saw his sister splashing in the water. It was only a few feet deep, but she couldn't swim. Her wet dress was pulling her down.

Milton stumbled into the water and grabbed Sarena. She threw her arms around him, and he sat down hard. He wrapped his arms around her, struggling to his feet. By the time he reached the edge, his father was there to pluck them out.

The other girls stared wide-eyed. "We were just walking along the dam," one of them whispered.

Henry crouched next to his sobbing daughter. Her bonnet had fallen off, and he brushed the wet hair from her eyes. "Hush now, it's all right."

Fanny swooped down and snatched Sarena. "Get away from her! You and your dam." As she strode toward the house, she called over her shoulder, "Come, Milton."

Henry met Milton's eyes. "Good work, my boy. Run along now and change your clothes."

Milton changed into dry clothes and then joined his mother by Sarena's bedside. His

sister lay under a mountain of blankets, although the afternoon was warm. "You should get in bed too," Fanny said.

Milton gazed down at Sarena. "I'm all right."

Fanny settled back in her rocking chair and gathered Milton onto her lap. She hugged him tight and kissed his forehead. Milton snuggled close, enjoying the unusual show of affection. Aunt Mattie pulled another chair near them.

"Has everybody gone?" Fanny asked.

Mattie wrinkled her nose. "The men headed into Nine Points for a drink at McComsey's hotel. The women have gone home."

Fanny's rocking soothed Milton, but he wished he didn't hear her next words. "I have had about enough. I swear, if that man does not make a success of himself soon, I am going to leave him."

Scarlet Fever

Spring rains filled the pond, and the trout grew. A pleasant summer turned to autumn. Winter came on mild, a relief in the drafty cabin that never stayed warm. But then disaster struck.

It had started as a little cold, with a sore throat and fever. Lots of the children at school had the same thing. Milton had spent several days at home with a cough. But while he quickly got better, Sarena, who was almost five, had gotten worse. A faint red rash started on her neck and spread down her chest and body. She complained that her stomach hurt, and she couldn't keep food down. Her tongue swelled and turned bright red.

They knew she had the deadly scarlet fever.

Milton ran up the steps to the house and pushed through the door. His father sat in the living room smoking a pipe. "How was school?" he asked.

"All right," Milton said. "How is she?"

Henry turned his gaze to the next room, but didn't speak. Milton ran into the kitchen. They had moved Sarena's bed beside the hearth, to keep her warm. Fanny sat next to the bed, praying.

Milton crept up beside her. "I came right home," he whispered. He didn't like school, anyway. The teacher was dull, and it was hard to pay attention. He had to sit on a long bench with four other squirming, whispering boys and whenever the teacher turned his back, the boys pushed one another until someone fell off. Sometimes Milton thought it was funny, but not today. Not with Sarena so sick.

Sarena burst out coughing. Milton started forward, but his mother's hand shot out to hold him back. "Let me," she said. "You keep away, so you don't catch it as well."

Fanny slipped her arm under Sarena's shoulders and propped her up. "Try to swallow some medicine, darling," she murmured, holding the bottle to Sarena's lips.

Henry tiptoed over. "Here's some more willow bark tea," he said softly.

Fanny snatched the cup away from him. She didn't seem to notice when hot water splashed on her hand. "You keep out of here! This is your fault. This cold house, and not enough to eat, no wonder the children get sick."

Fanny brushed tears from her eyes and turned to Sarena with the tea, which eased all kinds of aches and pains. Henry sighed and crept out of the room.

Milton stared at Sarena. Her eyes looked dull, and she didn't seem to see anyone around her. He choked back tears and joined his father in the parlor.

He stood next to his father's chair. Henry put an arm around Milton. "You know it's not my fault," he said. "I wouldn't do anything to hurt Sarena."

Milton nodded.

Henry took a ragged breath. "If she should die. . . ."

Milton swallowed hard. His father had said the dreaded word. What would they do if she died? Sarena brought sunshine to the home. She could make all of them smile. They couldn't be a family without her.

After two weeks, the rash faded and Sarena seemed to get better. They dared to hope. But they knew the pattern with scarlet fever: Most victims improved before taking a final turn for the worse. For Sarena's sake, they tried to pretend she was getting healthy.

"Don't make me go to school," Milton

begged. "I want to be here for her."

Henry frowned. "An education is important. Do you know why I couldn't be a writer? I didn't have enough education. But you, my boy, could go to college. You could become the writer in the family."

Milton didn't want to disappoint his father, but he didn't want to be a writer. He could barely make out the words on the signs the teacher posted on the schoolroom wall: KNOWLEDGE IS POWER. DO YOUR BEST, ANGELS DO NO MORE. It didn't seem to matter how much he went to school, or how hard he tried. He struggled with reading, writing, and arithmetic. He often felt the smack of the teacher's ruler across his knuckles. Going to school only made Milton feel stupid.

"Stay home," Fanny said. She glared at Henry. "You put too much stock in book learning. Look where all your reading has gotten you. Shakespeare! Newspapers! What good have they done? Milton could become a farmer if you ever did enough work to teach him properly. He could own a business. He doesn't need college for that."

Seeing his father's frown, Milton whispered, "I'll go to school next week, Papa, I promise."

Milton sat as near to Sarena as he dared. "Good morning, sunshine," he sang to her. "Guess what? I get to stay home and spend all day with you!"

She sat up, nestled in pillows, and gave him a smile that almost broke his heart. "Hooray! Tell me a story."

Milton wracked his brains for something to entertain her. "Well, you know how the doctor comes, with his medicine?"

Sarena's nose wrinkled. "He's nasty, and his medicine is nasty. It tastes like . . . like toads!"

Milton grinned. "Worse than toads. Like toads, and dead fish, and sour milk, all together. It smells worse than the oil fields. Well, one time the doctor came to give me medicine. Only I didn't want it."

Sarena's eyes opened wide. "What did you do?"

"I wanted to escape. So I jumped out a window."

Sarena clapped. "You got away from the doctor!"

Milton gave her a sheepish grin. "Well, not really. I wasn't very smart. I jumped out of a second-floor window and broke my leg. Then I had to get medicine for my cough and for my broken leg both, and stay in bed for a month."

Sarena clapped a hand over her mouth to hide her giggles. "Poor Milton!"

Milton didn't go to school the next week at all. His father didn't even suggest he should. Sarena died on March 31, 1867, just as the spring flowers pushed through the soil and new leaves greened the trees. For weeks the Hersheys mourned. The house seemed empty, as if that one little girl had held all the life in it.

Soon after, school closed for the summer

so the farm children could help with planting. Milton could not even be happy about that. His father spent more time in the fields, but what he was doing was anyone's guess. Fanny held Henry responsible for Sarena's death and barely spoke to him. Only Aunt Mattie seemed to offer Fanny some comfort, and visited more often.

"What did I do to deserve such punishment?" Fanny wailed to her sister a week after Sarena's death. "My life is over. There is nothing for me now."

"Nonsense," Mattie said, looking straight at Milton. "You have your son. And we must make sure he turns into a proper man. We cannot trust his father to do the job."

When the berries ripened, Milton sold them, walking door to door in his bare feet. The berries were sweet, but Milton wondered if people bought them because they felt sorry for him. He got such looks of sympathy when they saw his sad face. Often he got a biscuit or roll as well, though he seldom wanted to eat.

Summer brought heavy rains. One morning Milton stared out the window as the ground turned soggy and the birds huddled in the trees. "Won't it ever stop?" he whispered. He had had enough of darkness and gloom.

Henry bent to look over Milton's shoulder. He spoke with a cheerfulness that sounded fake. "The rain is a gift! It will keep the brook full. Come on, let's go check. A little water won't hurt us."

They put on their overcoats and went out. Henry strode ahead with his long legs. Milton trailed behind, his eyes on the ground.

His father gave a cry of agony. Milton's head jerked up. He ran forward to where his father stood, staring at the dam.

The seven-foot-high wall had collapsed, spilling water and fish into the field. Some fish still gasped and writhed, while others lay still. Henry groaned and covered his face with his hands. "All that work for nothing." He gazed at the dead fish for several minutes, then slowly walked back toward the house.

Milton stared at a trout as big as his hand. Its mouth opened and closed in silent gasps. *Is this all there is?* he wondered. *Hard work and suffering and death?* He felt as though there was nothing to look forward to. Long, dull days at school, to become something he didn't want to be, or years of struggle against droughts, floods, and pests as a farmer. Wasn't there any place people could be happy?

He remembered Harrisburg, with its bustling market and cheerful streets. He remembered the candy shop filled with laughing people. He didn't care about becoming rich and famous, following his father's dreams. He didn't even care about being successful, like his mother wanted. He would be satisfied if he could just make people happy.

Milton scooped up a flopping trout and eased it into the trickling stream. The fish rested for a minute, then flicked its fins and moved to deeper water. Its sides shimmered like a rainbow.

Milton's First Job

Two years after Sarena's death, Milton still missed her, but the ache wasn't so bad. Life went on.

Milton bounced into the kitchen and greeted his mother and aunt. Mattie offered her cheek for a kiss. "You are cheerful this morning."

Milton grinned. "No more school!"

"Milton is nearly fourteen now," his mother said proudly. "It is time for him to choose a career."

"You finally got your father to give up on

the idea of more schooling?" his aunt asked.

Milton shrugged. "We can't afford it." Henry Hershey was the only one who was disappointed about that. Milton did not add that his teacher thought he should leave. The teacher said that Milton would never learn anything.

Mattie gave Milton a glass of buttermilk. "So what will you do with yourself now?"

"Enjoy summer."

His aunt chuckled. "Isn't that just like a boy?"

"But you will have to make a decision soon," his mother said. "You are a man now."

Milton nodded, his mouth full of popover.

"I suppose you want to be a farmer, like your father," Aunt Mattie teased.

Fanny snorted and went back to making a broom. Milton shook his head. "I'd like to work in town, maybe as a shopkeeper." Visits to the city had always been a treat. How fun it would be to live there!

His aunt nodded. "That is respectable work. We will see what we can do for you."

Milton laughed. "No hurry." He was glad to be out of the one-room schoolhouse. He would no longer struggle to learn reading, writing, and arithmetic.

"When I'm a businessman, I'll buy you a house in the city," he told his mother. "And you won't have to work so hard anymore."

She smiled. "I wouldn't know what to do with myself if I didn't work. But I'll look forward to that house. Perhaps something with two stories, and a big wraparound porch?"

They built their dream house laughingly. Milton imagined it filled with all the latest gadgets. "We'll have gas put in, and lights in every room. No more carrying a lantern around! I'll get you one of those new carpet sweepers, and a washing machine with a hand crank."

Fanny shook her head. "I wouldn't know what to do with such things."

The door swung open and Henry Hershey strode in beaming. "Well, my boy, good news. I have found a job for you."

Milton stared at his father with his heart sinking. What kind of job would Henry think of as good?

Henry tossed his hat aside and sat at the table. "Yes, my boy, I only wish I had been so lucky at your age. You will be joining an honorable profession."

Milton forced himself to ask, "What is the job, Papa?"

"You, my boy, will be a printer's apprentice! Samuel Ernst has agreed to take you on." Henry leaned forward. "It is a perfect opportunity. If you work hard, you may yet become a writer or even a newspaper editor."

Milton wished his father would give up on that dream, for both of them. He knew his father and Mr. Ernst had a long-running argument about Henry's writing. Mr. Ernst said Henry's stories were not suitable for his religious readers. Henry took the criticism in his good-natured way, but he always held out hope that the next time would be different.

Why should Milton have a better chance? He didn't even have his father's storytelling skill. And the printer's shop was in Gap, a small town, not the bustling city. Still, it was a job away from the farm. It might not be so bad.

"Master Hershey!" Samuel Ernst roared.

Milton winced and stopped feeding paper into the printing press. He had been working for the printer for three months, and got yelled at nearly every day. *I should be used to it*, he thought. But he wasn't. He squared his shoulders and waited to find out what he had done wrong this time.

"I learned long ago that I could not trust you with the lettering," Samuel Ernst growled. "Now it seems you can not even do a simple task like running the press properly." He slapped a still-wet newspaper across the table. "Look at this! Does this look properly inked to you?"

Milton leaned forward to look. He had to admit, one corner of the paper was smeared with dark ink while in another corner the lettering was too light to read. "I'm sorry, sir."

"Sorry! An apprentice is supposed to help my work, not cost me money. Start over." Samuel Ernst stormed off.

Milton sighed and went back to work. He hated everything about the shop. He hated the smell of the ink. He hated the heat that made sweat pour down his back. He hated the noise of the press. Most of all, he hated his boss. And it was obvious that Samuel Ernst hated him.

With his fourteenth birthday approaching, a long, dreary future stretched before Milton. He worked twelve hours or more each day, six days a week. Milton didn't like the work, and his boss's temper made things worse. He couldn't even get away at night. He lived on the Ernst farm and did chores in the evening. Yet he couldn't simply quit and walk away. His father had signed a contract binding Milton to the printer for five years. Then he would be eighteen, and on his own, with all the skills needed to be a printer. But what good would that do him, when he didn't want to be a printer?

Milton started the press again and stared at it blankly. He had only one hope for escape. He could not end the apprenticeship agreement, but Samuel Ernst could. Milton would have to get Samuel Ernst to fire him.

What could he do to convince Mr. Ernst to let him go? He had made many little mistakes. But those just made Mr. Ernst yell at him. Milton didn't want to do anything too serious, like break the press. He didn't want to cost Mr. Ernst a lot of money, or get someone hurt. And he didn't want Mr. Ernst to have him arrested for a crime. Milton would have to make whatever he did look like an accident.

If he was rude enough, that might work. But Milton didn't think he could be that rude. He was too well trained in being polite. He fed sheets of paper into the press as he thought. Each piece of paper had to be fed by hand. It was one of the dullest jobs in the shop. It was also tricky. If you didn't feed the paper in evenly, it didn't print properly. It could even jam. Mr. Ernst yelled a lot when the paper got jammed.

Milton paused to lift his hat and wipe the sweat from his forehead. He fed the next sheet of paper in. He was so busy thinking that he almost caught his sleeve in the press. Milton jerked back. That would be dangerous. But it gave him an idea, and he started to smile.

Milton looked around the shop. Mr. Ernst was checking the typesetting with another apprentice. A third boy was bundling up the dry newspapers. No one was watching Milton.

He fed a sheet of paper into the printer. Then he lifted his hat again as if to wipe his forehead. He gave the hat a little flick and it fell forward. With a quick push, Milton fed it into the printing press.

"Oh, no! My hat!"

The others turned. The printing press spat out the straw hat, flattened and mangled. Bits of straw stuck to the press. Milton hid a smile.

Mr. Ernst stormed over. "Useless boy! What have you done now?" He scowled at the printing press. "Look at that! We will have to stop the printing, open up the press, and clean up all that straw. Then the press must be oiled and inked again." He turned his glare on Milton. "This is the last straw."

He didn't notice his pun. Milton almost chuckled, but he turned it into a cough. "It

was an accident," he grumbled, and waited a little too long before adding, "sir."

"Sorry isn't good enough," Mr. Ernst said. "You're fired."

"Yes, sir."

Milton gathered his things and strolled out of the print shop, smiling.

A Better Place

Milton's good mood faded as he neared home. Would his father be angry? Would his mother think he was starting down his father's path? Milton knew that most people thought Henry Hershey was a failure.

His mother had been disappointed so often. Milton could not bear to disappoint her again. He didn't care about getting rich, but he wanted his mother to have an easier life. And if he should ever marry someday, his wife should be comfortable too. In any case, Milton did not want to go back to living on the farm. He wouldn't spend his days on farm chores, seeing his father's failure and hearing his parents argue. He wanted more from life than that.

"I must get a new job this week," he said out loud. "I will work hard. I can be successful, if I just find the right job."

Milton took a deep breath as he walked up to his front door. He smiled as he entered and called out, "Hello! I'm home."

Fanny hurried into the kitchen, wiping her hands on her apron "Milton! What are you doing here?" She gave him a hug. "It is wonderful to see you, and just in time for dinner. Did Mr. Ernst give you the evening off?"

Milton led his mother to a chair and sat her down. "I have some bad news and some good news," he said gently. "The bad news is that Mr. Ernst has fired me." He gave a shaky smile. "And the good news is that Mr. Ernst has fired me."

His mother stared, and he went on quickly:

"Don't worry, I'll find another job soon. But I could not work there any longer. Mr. Ernst is a tyrant."

After a minute, his mother nodded. "That was never the place for you. We will find you something better."

Milton breathed a sigh of relief.

They were seated around a table with a cup of raspberry leaf tea when Henry came home. He did not take the news so well. "What! You cannot give up so easily. I will go to see Mr. Ernst tomorrow. Perhaps he will give you another chance."

Milton didn't know what to do. He could hardly tell his father that he had dropped his hat in the press on purpose. He could only hope that Mr. Ernst was too angry to relent.

With a sinking heart he watched his father ride off the next morning. His mother put a hand on his shoulder. "Do not worry. We will find a better position for you. Perhaps Mattie will have an idea. She should be here soon."

When Mattie arrived, Milton and his mother explained the situation to her. His aunt did not mind that he had lost his job. "I heard that they are looking for a boy at Royer's Ice Cream Parlor. You might do very well there."

Milton felt like the sun was rising inside him. He couldn't even speak for joy at the thought. If only Mr. Royer would take him on! Royer's Ice Cream Parlor and Garden was the best confectionery store in Lancaster. It produced the finest candies and ice cream. Surely Milton could be happy working someplace like that.

"We will go to see him as soon as your father gets back with the horse," Fanny said.

But when Henry returned, he strode in with a smile that made Milton's heart sink again. "Good news!" he boomed. "Mr. Ernst has agreed to give you another chance."

Tears came to Milton's eyes. He did not want to go back!

"Forget Mr. Ernst," Fanny said. "Milton can

do better than that. Mattie says that Mr. Royer is looking for a boy for his ice cream parlor. We will see if he will take Milton."

Henry gaped at her. "An ice cream parlor! You think that's better work than a newspaper? Boiling sugar and making candy! What kind of job is that for a man?"

"It seems to me that Mr. Royer and all his workers are men," Mattie said. "Mr. Royer is successful and well respected."

"But, Milton," Henry insisted, "just think what you could do as a newspaper editor! You could change how people think. You could help to create a better future."

"Milton does not want to be a printer," Fanny said. "His failure is your own fault for placing him there. Let us hear no more about it."

"But, Milton, my boy . . ." Henry gazed at Milton's face and trailed off with a sigh. "All right, go ahead and see Mr. Royer. You could do worse."

Fanny stood up. "Let us go see Mr. Royer right now. You do not want the job to go to someone else."

They all piled into the wagon and headed for Lancaster. On the journey Milton's feelings alternated between hope and fear. What if Mr. Royer had already hired someone? What if he would not take Milton? But if he did, what joy!

Milton found himself smiling as they turned down busy West King Street in the center of town. Well-dressed people strolled along, the women using pretty parasols against the sun. Royer's had a shaded terrace where customers crowded around small tables.

"Perhaps this will not be so bad after all," Henry said. "You're just around the corner from the Fulton Opera House. You can attend their lectures. I have heard that Mark Twain is coming this year! I'm sure many people will stop here after shows. You can make good connections."

Milton did not care about connections. He simply wanted to work someplace as exciting and wonderful as the ice cream parlor. He inhaled deeply as they entered the shop. His mouth watered at the smells of roasting nuts, baking pastry, and boiling caramels.

They found Mr. Royer, who looked Milton over carefully. "So you're interested in confectionery?"

"Yes, sir," Milton said. "I know I should love working here."

Mr. Royer smiled. "It is not all eating sweets. The work is hard, and very physical. You are not a big lad."

Milton tried to stand taller. "I am not afraid of hard work. I know I can do it if you give me the chance. I will do any job you say. I only want to learn."

"Very well." Mr. Royer held out his hand. "We will give you a try. Welcome to Royer's."

Milton shook Mr. Royer's hand, grinning from ear to ear.

"You will live above the shop," Mr. Royer said. "Your parents can bring your things out tomorrow. Here is an apron. You can get started right away."

"Yes, sir!" Milton said. He walked out with his parents and aunt to say good-bye.

"I know you will make us proud," Mattie said.

"Learn all you can," Henry said. "The city offers many opportunities."

Fanny hugged Milton. "It will be hard having you so far from home. At least the printer was nearby. I shall miss you."

Tears came to Milton's eyes. "I will miss you, too. I wish you lived here in Lancaster."

Fanny smiled. "Perhaps someday . . . someday soon. Now work hard and do your best to please Mr. Royer."

"I will! I promise I will do well."

The Candy Store

Milton sweated as he stirred sugar and water in a large cauldron. As the mixture started to boil, Milton had to keep it moving. He watched it closely, trying to judge the right moment to pull it off the heat. After a year at Royer's, fifteen-year-old Milton had experience with many types of candy. They often started with a vat of boiling sugar. That could become rock candy, lemon drops, lollipops, taffy, or soft candies. Stirring the mixture was hot work, and almost as hard as turning the crank on the huge ice cream maker.

"Now?" Milton asked.

Mr. Royer peered into the vat. "Yes, now!"

Milton and another apprentice grabbed the handles of the vat and poured the liquid onto a marble slab. Milton stepped back and wiped his brow. This batch would become taffy. It had to cool before the boys could pull it with hooks to make it soft and smooth.

"Nice work, Mr. Hershey," Mr. Royer said. "You have a good instinct for candy making."

Milton beamed. All his life he had struggled to memorize rules and facts. Making candy used experimentation and instinct. Milton was a natural with the tricky timing involved. He quickly learned how heat changed taste and texture. He was even learning to make the fanciest kinds of candy—marshmallows and individual chocolates.

"Better grab your dinner now," Mr. Royer said. "We'll be busy tonight."

Milton and another boy ran down the street

to an oyster house. They got six fried oysters for ten cents. Then it was back to Royer's to prepare for the evening rush. Milton didn't even mind working on a Friday night. The ice cream shop was the best place to be on a summer evening.

Milton darted between the tables, delivering dishes of ice cream and lemon pastry. Though normally shy, Milton found it easy to chat with customers. They were all so happy! Many young couples came on dates. Rugged farm laborers stopped by after the market. Milton also served rich city folk, theatergoers, and politicians from nearby city hall.

"Milton!" Mr. Royer called. "John Coyle is here. Step lively."

Milton smiled at a pair of pretty girls as he put down their desserts, then hurried out the front door. John Coyle was a young lawyer who often came to the ice cream shop with his dates. Milton greeted Coyle with a grin, admiring his handsome suit. Then he turned to see what pretty lady the popular lawyer had with him this time.

Coyle handed Milton the reins to his horse. "Take good care of her."

"Yes, sir!" Milton led the horse and carriage away from the door. He stroked the horse's head and neck and spoke softly to her. Another boy would find spots to tie up other customers' horses. But John Coyle was one of Mr. Royer's best customers, so he got special treatment. Milton was Coyle's favorite of the boys, for his gentle way with the horses. That meant Milton got pulled off his other duties for as long as John Coyle and his date were in the shop.

Milton enjoyed the cool evening air and the bustle of people passing. As much as he liked his work, it was nice to have these breaks. It seemed he was on the run from morning until night. He had learned so much! Mr. Royer taught him about buying ingredients, keeping inventory, and setting prices, as well as making candy. From watching his friendly employer, Milton had even learned about keeping customers and employees happy.

His mother had moved to a little house in the city. Aunt Mattie and Milton lived with her, but his father still lived in the country. Milton's mother often visited the ice cream parlor to make sure he was learning everything he could.

Finally John Coyle came out, and Milton held the horse while the young lawyer helped his date into the carriage. Coyle took the reins and climbed up to the seat. He tipped his hat to Milton and clucked at the horse. "Oh, wait!" he called with a grin. "I almost forgot." He flipped a dime to Milton, who caught it in the air. Mr. Coyle was one of the best tippers and Milton had learned to expect that dime.

On a different night, Milton and an apprentice named Felix closed up shop and headed to the Fulton Opera House to see a show. The boys sat in the gallery and laughed at the funny storyteller. As they left, Milton said, "That was fun. I'm glad we got here in time." He sniffed the air. "Do you smell peanuts?"

Felix lifted his nose. "Yes. It smells like the roaster. But we shouldn't be able to smell it from here."

The boys stared at each other. "You don't suppose . . ."

"We'd better go check," Felix said.

They dashed away from the opera house and turned down the street toward the ice cream shop. The boys stopped and stared. Thousands of peanut shells fluttered through the air.

A lady hurried by, shaking peanuts out of her hair. A gentleman paused to tip some off of his top hat. Several children ran around in the street, laughing and trying to catch the peanuts as they fell. More peanuts littered

the street, getting crushed under the hooves of passing horses.

The smell of roasting peanuts washed over them in waves. It was a wonderful smell, but Milton groaned, "We left the cooling fan on!"

They ran toward the shop. Milton fumbled for the key, pushed through the door, and hurried to the back room. He leaped for the fan and turned it off.

Milton and Felix gazed at the trays that had held roasted peanuts. Only a few nuts remained. Most had already blown up the flue and out to the street.

"Should we tell Mr. Royer?" Felix whispered.

Milton made a face. He remembered the "accident" with his hat in the printing press. What if Mr. Royer fired him, as Mr. Ernst had done? Still, Mr. Royer had been good to him, and Milton didn't want to lie. "We must tell him."

They found Mr. Royer at home. Once inside, Milton explained what had happened.

"All of the peanuts blew out into the street?" Mr. Royer asked, his eyes wide.

Milton and Felix nodded, their faces burning with shame. Mr. Royer scowled at them. His mouth twitched. And then he burst out laughing. The boys stared as Mr. Royer pulled out a handkerchief and mopped his streaming eyes.

"That must have been a sight to see!" Then Mr. Royer turned serious. "Well, my lads, I am sure you have learned your lesson. But you must make up for the loss of the peanuts. I will take it out of your wages."

Milton and Felix nodded. "Thank you, Mr. Royer!" they called as they left. Milton grinned with relief. Once again he knew that the ice cream shop was the perfect place for him.

Starting a Business

Henry Hershey threw down his paper. "Another millionaire! It seems like every day the newspaper has some story about a man who has made it big."

"But the whole country is in a recession," Aunt Mattie said. "All those railroads went out of business and so many foolish investors lost their stock."

Henry grinned at her. "See! I have taught you something about the world after all."

Aunt Mattie scowled and looked away.

Milton's father had moved into the house in Lancaster, after losing the farm. Milton was glad to have his father home again, but he quickly lost any hope that his parents would get along better. Neither had changed. Despite his latest failure, Henry was full of dreams. Fanny and her sister stood united against him.

Milton knew better than to try to make peace between them. He quietly ate his breakfast, thinking ahead to what he would do with this day off.

Henry went on. "Unemployment is high, and those who can find jobs work long hours in misery. Thousands of poor souls who work in the mines and factories die every year from the unsafe conditions." He tapped the paper. "And yet some men are still getting rich! I knew John Rockefeller when he was an ordinary speculator in the oil fields. But his family didn't make him leave. He stayed and became one of the richest men in America."

"His success was one out of thousands of failures," Fanny said. "And your destiny is to be one of the failures. You cannot recognize the value of hard work and sober living. Look at my family—they have money from farming, even now. The Snavelys saved enough to weather this recession. They are even buying up smaller businesses as they go under, and getting cheap land."

Henry frowned at his wife. "The workers will rebel against the selfish industrialists. The rich man has champagne, and the poor man can't even get beer."

"As you well know, my family does not drink alcohol," Fanny said. "Now are you going to sit here talking nonsense all day, or try to bring in a few pennies."

Henry rose and got his hat. "I am off to woo customers. Anything to please you, my dear." He left with a wink at Milton. He would spend the day selling picture frames and some of his own paintings. Many people in the area rejected all decorations as frivolous. With his charm, Henry did surprisingly well. But Milton knew his father would never get rich going door-to-door with his art.

Fanny turned to her sister and Milton and rubbed her hands together. "Now that he is gone, we can talk of serious matters. Milton, you have been with Mr. Royer for four years. You have learned all you can about making candy."

Milton nodded. "I can make everything that he sells. I still enjoy the work, but it is not so exciting without new things to learn. Sometimes Mr. Royer lets me experiment, but not often. The ingredients are too expensive."

"It is time you moved on to your own business," Fanny said. "You cannot be an apprentice forever. You are nearly nineteen."

Milton's heart beat faster. "I have saved a little money, but not enough to start in business."

Fanny and Mattie exchanged a look. Milton realized they had planned this already. "You have proven yourself capable of hard work," Mattie said. "The Snavelys will provide the money to get you started on your own."

Milton sat back and grinned. He enjoyed his work at the ice cream parlor, but now he could have more freedom! He could experiment with new recipes and turn out the best candy anywhere. He could see the customers' smiles, and know he was responsible.

"First we must settle one question," Mattie said. "What is the best location for the shop?"

Milton thought for a while. "It would be hard to compete against Mr. Royer here in Lancaster. He is already so popular. And I would feel bad trying to steal his customers." An idea was growing in him, but he hardly dared to express it. Most people never traveled more than a few miles from where they were born.

He took a deep breath. He remembered that childhood trip from the Titusville oil fields, and the exciting cities they had passed. "Perhaps Pittsburgh?"

Fanny and Mattie frowned in thought. Then Mattie slowly smiled. "No. The place to be is Philadelphia. The Centennial Exposition opens in May."

"The world's fair!" Milton whispered. It was the first world's fair held in America, celebrating the hundredth anniversary of the signing of the Declaration of Independence.

"Five great exhibit halls and hundreds of smaller buildings," Mattie said. "Thousands of workers, tens of thousands of visitors." She cackled. "The old coot is right—I *have* learned something from all of his ramblings over the newspaper!" She leaned forward across the table. "If you want to make money, you go where the money is. The money will be in Philadelphia at the fair."

The three grinned at one another. "I think

it is a very good idea," Fanny said. "My brothers have agreed to give you one hundred fifty dollars in starting funds."

Milton gasped. He imagined the store he could open, with a fine glass display case to show off his candies, and customers crowding around. Philadelphia was the second-largest city in America. It would be full of excitement, especially with the fair. Then Milton looked at his mother, and some of his joy faded. Philadelphia was a long way from home. "I shall miss you, though."

Fanny's eyes widened in surprise. "You don't think we would send you out there by yourself! I shall go with you, of course."

"I shall come too," Mattie said. "I have gotten used to seeing you both every day. I would not know what to do with myself here after you left."

Milton smiled his gratitude. "And Father?"

"We do not need him," Fanny said.

"My brothers are willing to lend the money

because Fanny and I have told them that you are reliable," Mattie said. "But your father is not to be trusted. He would only find a way to cause problems."

Milton wished his parents would reconcile, but that seemed more impossible than any of Henry's dreams.

Several months later, Milton left the Centennial Exposition with his mother. They had spent the day mostly in the Main Exhibition Building, with its displays from around the world. "Philadelphia has been even more wonderful than I hoped!" Milton said.

They returned to the narrow brick house they had rented on Spring Garden Street. It had a storefront with a kitchen in the basement, and a living area above. Aunt Mattie had provided tables and chairs brought by wagon from Lancaster. Milton had installed a stove and large copper kettle in the kitchen. He had already started making candies, selling them from a pushcart to the crowds outside the fair entrance. But he looked forward to June 1, 1876, the opening day of the Spring Garden Confectionery Works.

He gazed around the little shop with pleasure. "It is a pity we were not ready in time for the Exposition's opening day on May tenth. So many thousands of people passing by!"

"It is better to be prepared and do a thing right," his mother said. "In any case, the fair has created such a sensation that the crowds will keep coming."

Aunt Mattie came downstairs. "There you are! Your business cards are ready." She handed Milton a box, and he smiled at the cards. They read M.S. HERSHEY, DEALER IN FINE CONFECTIONERY, FRUITS, NUTS, &C. The center showed an engraving of the fair's Machinery Hall.

Fanny peered over his shoulder. "Don't you think a picture of something more natural and wholesome would have been better?"

Milton shook his head. "We are in the machine age. The Machinery Hall, with all the hundreds of machines on exhibit, is the most popular part of the fair. This card suggests that we have a big factory."

His aunt smiled. "Perhaps someday you will."

June 1 was a wonderful day for the opening. The weather was sunny and mild, staying light until past eight in the evening. Milton had installed a pipe in the coal chute to carry the sweet smell of candy from the kitchen out into the street. People who left the fair passed nearby as they headed for the city center. Many of them stopped in the Spring Garden Confectionery Works for candy, fruit, and nuts.

Milton kept running up from the kitchen. He gave customers a warm welcome. Fanny laughed. "Mattie and I can take care of the customers. You just keep that candy coming."

Milton grinned. "But down in the kitchen, I miss all the excitement! It is wonderful to see the shop such a success."

Fanny nodded. "If these crowds keep up, you will need to hire employees." She beamed at her son. "You have done it."

Money Trouble

On November 11, Milton wandered to the fair-grounds. His mother and aunt had returned to Lancaster for a rest, but Milton had hired other employees to staff the counter while he was in the kitchen. In any case, the shop would not draw crowds on such a cold, dreary day.

Not like the previous night. Milton smiled as he remembered the crowds who came for the Centennial's closing celebration, with its fireworks show. But, now. . . . Milton sighed.

Would his business succeed without the fairgrounds, and with winter coming?

He joined a group of boys and men standing outside the fairgrounds. They had come to watch the great buildings emptied. Workers carried boxes and machinery to waiting freight cars. "They're sending all that to the Smithsonian Institution in Washington," an older man said.

"It doesn't seem right," a teenage boy commented. "It should stay here in our city."

The first man shrugged. "We saw it first, anyway."

Milton moved closer to the men. He usually felt shy around strangers, but he wanted to share this sad moment with someone. "Those huge buildings held such wonderful things," he said. "Soon they will stand empty."

The older man turned his blue eyes and weather-beaten face to Milton. "Not for long. They are going to auction off all the buildings. The buyers will move them and turn them into businesses, train stations, and hotels."

"It's hard to imagine," Milton said, gazing at the enormous Machinery Hall building. "We live in a remarkable era. Did you see all those inventions? Mechanical calculators. An engine powered by gasoline. Sewing machines, lights, and even a telephone run by electricity!"

"Aye," the old man said. "It's not the world I grew up in. Everything is changing."

Milton heard the sadness in the old man's voice. He took one of his business cards out of his pocket. "Not everything. At the Spring Garden Confectionery Works, you can buy candy just like you had as a child! Stop by, and I'll give you a free sample of rock candy."

The teenage boy and his friends gathered around. Soon Milton had a group asking about his shop. "Come right now," he suggested. "This day could use some cheer."

A dozen men and boys followed him to the shop. Milton gave out samples of his less expensive candy. He wouldn't make money, but he enjoyed seeing the shop filled with smiles and laughter again. Perhaps some of these people would even return as regular customers.

A young boy, raggedly dressed, peered into the display case. "Are those chocolates? They look very fine."

"Yes," Milton said. "Each one is handmade. Working with chocolate is tricky."

"I've never had a chocolate before," the boy said.

Milton hesitated. Chocolates were expensive. Middle-class folks might sometimes have hot cocoa, or sugar candies with a thin coating of chocolate. But only the rich could easily buy the individual chocolate candies.

Milton looked at the men and boys enjoying his hard candies and candied fruit. None of them looked rich. Most were probably out of work, if they had nothing to do but watch the fairgrounds empty. If he gave this poor boy a

chocolate, he should offer some to the others as well. That would cost him a lot of money. But it didn't seem fair that only the rich should enjoy such a treat. He remembered his father saying, "The rich man has champagne, and the poor man can't even get beer."

Milton went behind the display case and pulled out the tray of chocolates. He held it in front of the boy. "Choose one. Everyone should get a taste of chocolate sometime in his life!" The boy's face lit up as he reached for the treat. Milton knew he had made a good choice.

To Milton's relief, his business grew over the next two years. Fanny and Mattie moved back to help wrap candies. They moved the store a few doors down, to a larger space. They even opened a wholesale shop in another part of town. There they sold wrapped candy to other stores. In the summer of 1878, business was bustling.

Milton experimented with new recipes whenever he had time. Fanny scolded him. "The most popular candies have been around for generations. Why should you waste ingredients on experiments that might fail?"

"This city has hundreds of candy shops," Milton said. "We must make ourselves stand out from the crowd. If I make something new and special enough, we could be famous."

"You are starting to sound like your father," Fanny said. "But at least you work for your dreams." She patted his shoulder and left him to work.

Inventing was Milton's favorite part of the job. Perhaps he was like his father in that way. He experimented with caramels. He added a little more of this ingredient and a little less of that one. He cooked them at higher or lower temperatures, for shorter or longer times.

Finally he finished a batch that satisfied him. He let the caramels cool, and chewed one slowly. The flavor was delicious. It was also softer than other caramels, so it didn't stick to the teeth quite so much. He put a few on a dish and headed upstairs.

He smiled at the pretty shopgirls staffing the front counter. Sometimes he wished he had the nerve to ask one of them for a date. But it would not be right, since he was their employer. Besides, his mother would not approve.

Milton approached some customers, two young couples who came at least once a week. "Pirates!" one of the men was saying. "Can you believe that? Real pirates attacked a schooner anchored in the Delaware River. You'd think we were living in the eighteenth century."

His date looked up at Milton. "Good afternoon, Mr. Hershey. What do you have there?"

"My latest creation! I thought you might like to be the first customers to try it." He handed around the soft, chewy caramels and held his breath while the young people started chewing.

For a full minute, no one spoke. Then the young woman swallowed and said, "Oh, my! That was . . . it was. . . ." She shook her head.

Milton gazed at her anxiously. He had worked on this recipe for weeks, and thought the caramels very fine. Had he been wrong?

The other young woman looked up with her eyes shining. "Delicious!"

"Wonderful," one of the men said. "The best I've had. It doesn't stick in your teeth like most caramels."

The first young woman opened her purse. "Do you have more? Because I want to take some home today. My little brothers will adore them."

Milton beamed. "I'll have one of the girls wrap some up for you."

He hurried to the back room. His mother and aunt were wrapping candies to send to the wholesale outlet. He grabbed his mother in a hug.

"Milton! What on earth?"

"My new caramels! They are a success. I told you!" He danced around the room.

Fanny and Mattie laughed. "All right, son," Fanny said. "Bring us some and we will wrap them for the wholesaler to try. But if this is the success you imagine, you will have to hire some helpers for us. Mattie and I can hardly keep up with the demand now!"

The caramels were a success, and for a while the business thrived. But by late 1879, Milton was running out of money. He struggled to increase income.

"How do we go through so much?" he wondered aloud. "Our sales are high, but we cannot seem to make a profit. The ingredients just cost so much—the price of sugar is up again, and fresh milk is so expensive here in the city."

"You must raise the prices," Fanny said.

Mattie shook her head. "That won't do. The wholesale office has hundreds of other candy sellers to choose from. We must keep our prices low to compete."

"But our product is better," Fanny said.

"Perhaps," Mattie said, "but people do not have money to spare. Times are still bad."

Milton sighed. "We must carry on as well as we can."

Milton struggled to balance his account books, but things only got worse. By October of 1880, he was desperate for help.

"It is my own fault," he said to his mother and aunt. "No matter how hard I try, I cannot make the numbers add up properly. I never was good with arithmetic."

Fanny peered at the account books. "I can make no sense of it. Accounting is men's work." She looked up at Milton. "We must hire someone who can help."

Mattie said, "Do you remember Mr. Lebkicher in Lancaster? He is a Civil War veteran, and a good businessman. Perhaps he could be persuaded to come help us."

Milton and Fanny gazed at her hopefully. "Do you really think he would come?" Milton asked.

"Let us write to him at once."

William H. "Harry" Lebkicher accepted the job. He was about as old as Milton's father, but a much better businessman. Unfortunately, he had only bad news for Milton.

"You need more money, a great deal of money, right away. You need to pay off your sugar and milk suppliers."

"But without the ingredients, I cannot make candies!" Milton wailed. "We do good business during the holidays, but I must have the supplies. If only they will give me more time."

"They will not provide any more credit," Mr. Lebkicher said. "You need about six hundred dollars."

Milton gasped. That was twice what an average worker made in a year!

"I do not see how you can possibly get enough money unless you can borrow it," Mr. Lebkicher said.

Milton looked at his mother and aunt. He could feel their disappointment. How had he gotten the shop into such trouble? Perhaps if he had done better with arithmetic in school . . . but it was too late for that.

Aunt Mattie sighed. "You must write to my brothers. Tell them I have said they should give you the money."

Milton nodded. He understood what his aunt did not say. His uncles would hesitate to lend money to Milton, for fear he was turning into his father. And they would not give money to Fanny, since a husband owned his wife's property. But Mattie had great standing in the family. Since she had never married, her brothers were still responsible for her. Perhaps they would do as she asked.

He struggled over the wording of the letter. Once again, he felt frustrated by his poor education. But at least he thought he got the message across.

Dear Uncle

I am sorry to bother You but cannot well do without as it takes so much money. Just Now aunt Martha wishes You to send 600 dollar . . . and she will stand good for it. She just want it till the first of the Year, so you will greatly oblige Me by send it as sune as possible on Monday and do not fail as it will save us some trouble.

Respet Nephew

Milt

Martha Snavely

Aunt Mattie added her own note:

I will write Some othr time

While they waited for the reply, Milton wondered if they would have to close the shop.

More Struggles

Everyone breathed a sigh of relief when the money finally came. It carried them through Christmas. But a few months later, the store was running out of money again.

"Sugar is getting more expensive all the time," Harry Lebkicher said. "And the Franklin Sugar Company has such tight credit terms."

"They demand payment at once, but my wholesale customers take months to pay me," Milton complained. "We need sugar more than anything. Even though we are selling well, we never seem to have enough money."

"You must look for anyplace you can cut costs," Mr. Lebkicher said. "I suggest you stop selling cakes. You don't make much profit off of them, and they spoil too quickly."

Milton gazed at the decorated cakes in the case. They looked so pretty. But he nodded. Staying in business required tough decisions.

"The wholesalers will take even more candies," Fanny said, "but we don't have the space to make them."

"I will look for a new location," Mr. Lebkicher said. "But the move will take money. Do you think the Snavely brothers . . . ?"

Milton looked at his aunt Mattie. She said, "Write to them at once, and tell them I am making a large new investment in the shop."

Milton touched her hand gratefully. "I do not know what I would do without you."

Mr. Lebkicher smiled at Mattie. "Milton is

lucky to have an aunt who is so generous and wise. Would you like to accompany me as I scout new locations?"

"Very well," Mattie said. Mr. Lebkicher offered her his arm, and they left the store.

Fanny gazed after them thoughtfully. "He would ask her to marry him, if he got the chance. But she is not interested."

"I thought every woman wanted to get married," Milton said. "Don't you sometimes miss having a husband around?"

"Never. I have your interests to keep me busy. That is enough. It is enough for Mattie as well. You are like a son to her, too."

Milton sighed. He depended on his aunt, and was grateful for her interest. But he did miss his father, and wished they could be a family again.

Milton's uncles sent enough money to pay for the move. The new shop was bigger, but cost less to rent. Milton started to feel that he could

115

make the business work, if he was careful.

The summer of 1881 seemed unbearably hot. Much of the candy softened or melted in the cases. At least ice cream sold as fast as they could make it.

One afternoon the waitress burst into the kitchen where Milton was working. "Oh, Mr. Hershey!"

"Yes? Is everything all right?"

The girl's gaze flicked to Fanny, then back to Milton. "Your father is here, sir."

Milton wiped his hands and followed the girl, grinning. He found his father leaning against the display case. The girl who worked behind the counter was laughing at something he'd said.

Milton hurried forward. "Papa!"

"It is wonderful to see you, my boy." Henry embraced him, then stepped back. "You have become a fine young man."

The two men gazed at each other. Milton was short and stocky, with aqua blue eyes and a thick dark mustache that helped him feel older. His father's hair and beard were going gray, but he still stood tall and elegant in his worn silk suit.

"I am so glad you could visit," Milton said. "What brings you to the city?"

"My latest creation!" Henry gestured to something sitting on the counter. For the first time, Milton noticed the glass and wood cabinet. It was beautiful, with shiny brass fittings. The front was divided into many panes of glass.

"It sits on the counter," Henry said. "You can show off different candies in each section." He went behind the counter and smiled at the girl there. "Hand me a tray of caramels, my dear." She did, and he slid them into the back of the case. "You see, these little boards slide down from the top and hold the candies in place. That way the case always looks full. A clerk can open the cabinet from the back to serve customers."

"It is very nice." Milton looked up to see his mother and aunt watching them. "Wasn't it nice of Father to bring us this display case?"

His mother didn't speak.

Henry glanced up and smiled. "Ah, Fanny, my dear!" He started toward her with his hand outstretched, but she folded her arms and stepped back. Henry stopped and gave a small bow. "And you, Mattie? You are looking very well."

"What are you up to now, you old rascal?" Mattie asked.

"I am going into business with Milton," Henry said cheerfully. "We will sell my patented cabinets to other shops around town. I have an idea for cough drops that are sure to be wildly popular. We will sell them with the cabinets. We can invest the profits with a man I know, who is going to turn wire fences into telephone lines."

Milton remembered the electric telephone displayed at the fair. "Will that work?"

"Of course not," Fanny said. "Nothing your father does works."

"Now, Mother," Milton protested.

"It is quite all right," Henry said with a little bow. "My wife has always been a skeptic. But you must dream big, to make big things happen." He shifted his cabinet to a prominent place on the counter. "We might as well start filling this right now. You will double your sales in no time." The clerk started helping Henry.

Mattie pulled Milton aside. "You must not give into that man's demands! He will ruin the business."

"But, Auntie," Milton pleaded. "I cannot just turn him away. He is my father. In any case, the cabinet is very nice. It may do well."

Mattie sighed. "That man has the curse of failure upon him. We must go carefully."

Bang!

Milton awoke from a sound sleep. He lay in

the dark, listening, trying to figure out what had woken him.

Bang! Bang! It sounded like an explosion, like fireworks going off. Milton slid from his bed and fumbled for his dressing robe. He met the others in the hallway. "That came from the kitchen," Aunt Mattie said.

Milton's heart raced as he hurried for the kitchen. Had something gone wrong with the equipment? He was sure he had turned off everything properly. He had not been careless since the time the peanuts flew out the air vent at Royer's.

In the kitchen he lit the gas lantern with a shaking hand. What was that strange, sour smell? The equipment looked all right, but as he turned up the lantern, he saw red splashes on the walls.

"What in heaven's name?" Fanny gasped. Milton could only stare.

Mattie strode forward. She dipped a finger in the red goop splattered across the ice cream machine and sniffed it. "Tomatoes! Fermented tomatoes!" She flicked the stuff off of her finger and strode toward Henry with her fists clenched. "This is your fault, you irresponsible, scatterbrained fool!"

Milton covered his face with his hands and groaned. His father had sworn that this scheme of canning vegetables would make a fortune. But it looked like another costly failure. Henry always managed to make his ideas sound wonderful, and Milton could never say no. But all of Henry's ideas cost money, and so far, that money had just disappeared.

The cabinets had not sold well. Henry's cough drop was not the success he had predicted. Competition was stiff, they did not have enough money for a large ad campaign, and now it looked like their entire stock of canned vegetables was ruined. Once again, the shop was leaking money like water.

"I will clean up the mess," Henry said with dignity.

"That is not the point!" Fanny yelled. "We were doing fine until you arrived. Now it is one disaster after another. And each one expensive!"

As their argument raged, Milton started to feel dizzy. He groped for something to hold on to. He leaned against the stove, which was still warm from the day's work. For weeks he had been feeling poorly. His heart often raced and thudded in his chest. His stomach hurt, so he could only eat bland foods. His breath wheezed in his chest. Sometimes his hands shook as he tried to make the candy.

He felt a hand on his arm. "We will handle things here," Aunt Mattie said. "You must get back to bed."

Heading West

Milton could not rise from bed the next morning. His mother called for a doctor.

"He has suffered a mental breakdown," the doctor said. "He is very ill, and must have complete rest."

Fanny turned to Henry and hissed, "This is your fault!"

"But I have only tried to help!"

Milton turned his face to the wall. The doctor pushed the others out of the room. "He must have quiet, and no stress."

But how could he be free of stress, when his business was failing? He trusted Aunt Mattie and Mr. Lebkicher to do their best, but could they do enough? And even from his bedroom, Milton could hear the fights that raged through the house. He didn't want to tell his father to go. Yet he had to admit, life was harder when he was around.

A couple of weeks later, Henry came in and sat by Milton's bed. Henry looked tired, with more lines on his face than he'd had six months before. The time had been hard on him, too. But when he smiled at Milton, the old twinkle lit his eyes. "How are you feeling, my boy?" he asked gently.

Milton sighed. "I wish I could go back to work. But the doctor says it is too dangerous. I must stay in bed."

Henry nodded. He gazed into the distance for a minute. Finally he said, "The newspapers have reported finding silver out West. I have a mind to seek my fortune there."

Milton didn't speak. Though he loved his father, a wave of relief washed over him.

"If I had enough money to stake my own mining claim, I would go at once," Henry said. "You could buy out my share of the cabinet business for three hundred and fifty dollars."

Milton closed his eyes for a minute. The business could not afford to lose another $350. Yet they could also not afford to keep Henry around, with his crazy, expensive schemes. And he could not send his father away with nothing. Finally he opened his eyes and nodded. "I will ask Mr. Lebkicher to pay you the money. And I wish you the best of luck in the West."

With his father gone, the business ran more smoothly. Milton quickly recovered. Unfortunately, business didn't.

"It is hopeless," he wailed, going over the books one more time with Mr. Lebkicher.

Mr. Lebkicher agreed. "I don't see how we

can keep going without another loan."

They both looked at Aunt Mattie. She nodded. "With that man gone, we can finally make this shop a success. Write to my brothers for more money."

Milton wrote three letters before he got a response. Finally a little money came, but not enough to pay off their debts. Throughout that year, the shop struggled. And then Milton's pleas for more money went unanswered. Mattie traveled to Lancaster to see her brothers in person.

When her carriage pulled up outside the shop again, Milton ran to greet her. He took the reins and looped them over the hitching post, anxiously watching her face.

"Hello, Milton," Mattie said, and gave him the barest smile. His heart sank.

They went into the store together and joined Fanny and Mr. Lebkicher. "I'm sorry, Milton," Mattie said. "Abraham and Benjamin say they will send no more money. They say their funds are tied up in other businesses. They have no more to lend."

They sat silent for a full minute. Finally Milton whispered, "Then what are we to do?"

Mattie sighed. "My brothers advise you to close the shop and sell the equipment. Then you might have money to start again somewhere else. Someplace less expensive and less competitive. Perhaps coming to such a large city wasn't the best choice after all."

Milton looked at Mr. Lebkicher, hoping for another answer. "I am afraid I can suggest nothing better," he said. "We must make plans to close the shop."

In March of 1882, two of Milton's cousins arrived. They brought a big wagon pulled by two giant draft horses. They entered the shop and gazed at the bare tables and empty display case. Henry's fancy cabinet stood on the counter.

"Hello Stoner, hello Rohrer," Milton said.

They tipped their hats to him. "Afternoon, Milton."

Then Stoner said, "Well, we'd best get to work. Show us the kitchen."

They worked in the same slow, steady manner that Milton remembered from his childhood. In a few hours, they had dismantled the kitchen completely. The copper candy kettles and other equipment sat in the wagon.

"Ready to go?" Stoner asked.

Milton's eyes stung with unshed tears. "I will join you in a minute," he whispered.

His cousins nodded and went to wait with the wagon. Milton turned back to Fanny, Mattie, and Mr. Lebkicher.

"Don't worry," Mr. Lebkicher said. "We will finish up here, and then I will see that your mother and aunt head safely back to Lancaster."

"Are you sure you won't join us?" Milton asked.

Mr. Lebkicher took a long look at Mattie, but then he shook his head. "I have gotten used to the city. But I wish you the best of luck."

Milton looked around the shop. "Six years! Six years of my life, and all for nothing."

Mattie stepped forward and took his arm. "Don't talk like that. You have worked hard and learned from your mistakes. You will get another chance."

Milton hugged her, and then his mother. He shook hands with Mr. Lebkicher. Then he joined his cousins on the driver's seat of the wagon. He had plenty of time to think of his losses on the long trip back to Lancaster.

Milton didn't know what to do with himself in Lancaster. He felt uncomfortable under the watchful eyes of his uncles. They had no interest in anything but business, and didn't know how to laugh. They didn't bring up their lost money. Still, Milton felt their disapproval every time they looked at him. He understood how his father must have felt all those years. Now Milton was also a failure, a disappointment, to the Snavelys.

A letter arrived from Henry. Colorado was wonderful, he said. The West was filled with opportunities. A man could get rich, and have fun doing it.

Milton put down the letter and thought. He doubted prospecting would make Henry's fortune, or his own. But a visit to the West had appeal. He would get away from his uncles. He had been working too hard, and could use a change. His doctor had even suggested that the dry air of the West might help his lungs. He could have some adventures—the kind of adventures a young man should have. His mind filled with the stories he had heard as a boy, of cowboys and Indians, gunfights and saloons.

Milton felt lighter after making his decision. He knew his mother and aunt wouldn't like it. They would prefer he never saw his father again. But they would understand his decision to go away.

"That's it," Milton said. "I am going west."

Drama in Denver

Milton got off the train at Denver's Union Station. He gazed at the long, three-story building with lots of arched windows. The station looked like an East Coast mansion, not like anything from the Wild West. Milton felt oddly disappointed.

He walked through the station and turned onto a sidewalk made of boards. Buggies pulled by horses crowded the wide, dirt street. People filled the sidewalks, mostly men in suits and hats.

A man came up to Milton. "Hey, are you interested in a lottery ticket? It's a sure thing. Only one dollar, and you could win a hundred."

"No, thank you." Milton had learned about enough "sure things" from his father.

He walked toward a cluster of people. They were gathered around a man who was standing up on a box.

The man held up his hand. "I have here a ten-dollar bill." He wrapped the money around a small piece of soap. Then he wrapped a piece of paper around the money. He dropped it onto a pile of similar papers at his feet. "Pick a piece out of the pile, for just one dollar! You could earn nine dollars for your investment. Who wants to try it first?"

A young man pushed forward. He was dressed well, and he had a suitcase. Milton recognized him from the train. "I'll give it a go."

He reached for a paper bundle. "I saw just where you dropped it." He tore off the paper. Milton craned his neck to see.

"What? But I was so sure!" The young man stared at a piece of soap.

Another man patted him on the shoulder. "Tough luck. But why waste your time over that kind of money, anyway? You can just get to the mining and mineral investment office before they close. And then, perhaps, a game of poker tonight. I'll show you where."

Milton watched them walk away. A couple of older gentlemen glanced at the man with the soap. One of them murmured, "He's still getting them with that old trick. Anyone could see it's just sleight of hand."

Milton hurried away. At least he hadn't been fooled by that trick!

He passed a law office, a fur company, and a dry goods store. He stopped to gaze at the Windsor Hotel, a large building built of tan and gray stone. Milton turned away. Of course his father would not be staying in a place as nice as that.

He kept going until he found the Arcade, which his father had listed as his address. Milton was not too surprised to find that the Arcade was a saloon. But a sign near the door advertised SINGLE ROOMS 20C A NIGHT, 1.00 A WEEK.

A group of men lounging outside the Arcade watched him. One stepped forward and said, "Hey there, friend, are you looking for a card game?"

Milton shook his head. "I am looking for my father, Mr. Henry Hershey. Do you know him?"

The man smiled. "I expect he is inside. Come on in."

Milton followed the man but stopped just inside the doors. Men sat around tables, most with their jackets off but their hats still on. Smoke filled the air from the cigars and cigarettes.

"How about some three-card monte?" The man tried to drag Milton forward.

135

"No, sir," Milton said. "I am here to find my father and that is all." He pulled away and found the lodging rooms. His father had a small room on the top floor.

Henry greeted Milton with an embrace. "Milton, my boy, so you made it! Now we shall take Denver by storm."

Milton sat on one of the narrow, creaking beds. "This city seems full of tricksters."

Henry nodded. "Soapy Smith is the leader of them all. They call the lower part of downtown the Streets of Doom. They say if you can get from Union Station to Larimer Street without losing any money, then you're safe from the Soap Gang. Mostly safe, anyway."

Milton frowned. His father might have mentioned this in one of his letters! "Should I know of any other dangers? I assume the Indians do not cause trouble here in the city."

"The Indians are gone," Henry said. "The army has won the Indian Wars, and last year they sent the Ute tribe to Utah. No, the things to watch out for now are disease, tricksters, and thieves. Why, just after I arrived, Buffalo Bill had two thousand dollars' worth of jewelry stolen from his hotel room!"

Milton slipped a hand into his pocket. He still had the money Aunt Mattie had given him—a hundred dollars. He would have to watch that carefully. "You have given up on silver mining, then?"

Henry nodded. "Leadville is a rough town. Denver has culture, even an opera house. It suits me better. For a while I sold livestock medicine in the countryside, but now I am painting pictures."

Milton said, "Tomorrow I will look for a job, and avoid those Streets of Doom."

Henry reached under his pillow and pulled out a gun. "Take this."

Milton stared at the gun. "I've never shot a revolver before! I would be no good in a gunfight."

"You won't be facing down a gunslinger in the streets," Henry said. "Real gunfights hardly ever happen anymore. Why, Ed Chase said that only once has a gun been shot off in his saloon. A drunk dropped his gun and it went off. Chase is a good man. He allows no cheating at the gaming tables. He gives food to the hungry, and money to widows and children."

"So why do I need a gun?" Milton asked.

Henry shrugged. "Sometimes it is helpful to let people know you are serious. Go ahead and take it."

"Very well." Milton carefully took the gun and slipped it into his coat pocket. But he was sure he would never use it.

The next morning, Milton wandered the streets of Denver. He headed away from the train station. The con artists hung around there, because that's where new people came into town.

Milton stopped inside a few businesses to see if they needed help, but no one was hiring. Eventually, he came upon the big, modern buildings and then an area of rundown shacks. He was just about to turn back when he saw a HELP WANTED sign.

Milton peered down the narrow alley at the drab shack. He could not even tell what kind of business it was. The muddy alley stank of garbage, and a stray cat hissed at Milton. He thought of leaving, but this was the first HELP WANTED sign he had seen. He might as well find out about the job.

He knocked on the door, and someone called, "Come in."

Milton stepped inside the small room and peered around in the dim light. An old man with dirty clothes and a tangled beard was sprawled on a couch.

"I saw your sign . . . ," Milton began.

The old man pointed toward another door. "Go in that back room, with the other boys."

Milton crossed the room and opened the other door. He saw three young men seated on boxes around an old table, playing cards. They wore rough clothes and smoked cigarettes. They looked up at him with hard eyes.

Milton did not like the look of things. He closed the door without going through and turned to the old man. "What kind of job is it?"

"Just go back there, and you will find out." He smiled in a way Milton did not like. "You want a job, don't you?"

Milton still had one hundred dollars in his pocket. He had been afraid to leave it in the lodging room. He did not need a job badly, and he did not trust any of these men. They might try to steal his money.

He walked back to the front door. He turned the handle, but it was locked.

Milton spun on the old man. "Let me out!"

The old man grinned at him. "I'm just helping you. You want a job. I need workers. We'll

send you out to the country to take care of livestock. It's hard work, but it will make a man of you. Don't worry—we'll let you come home in a year or two." He laughed.

Milton backed up against the door, his heart racing. How had he gotten himself into this? He knew that if he yelled for help, it would only make things worse. No outsiders would interfere, but the fellows in the next room might come after him. These kidnappers must send young men to work in some remote area, where they couldn't find their way back.

Milton remembered the gun in his pocket. He pulled it out and pointed it at the old man. He tried to make his voice hard. "You let me out at once."

The old man stared. Then he reached up and pulled a string. Without turning around, Milton reached for the door handle. It turned, and Milton backed out of the building.

With the door closed behind him, he shoved

the gun in his pocket and hurried down the alley. Why had he come to Denver? Why had he listened to his father's stories about how wonderful it was? He should know better by now!

By the time he neared the city center, Milton felt better. He had done well in a tight situation. Just wait until they heard about it back in Lancaster. He would have a good story to tell, anyway. Before he came, Milton had thought that he wanted adventures. Well, he had certainly gotten one!

Milton kept wandering through Denver. He glanced at signs for auction houses, investment offices, and gambling clubs. They could not fool him with their easy promises. He had avoided con men and kidnappers successfully, so far. He felt he could handle anything.

And then he saw a sign for a candy shop.

New Lessons

Milton thought he knew all about caramels, until he saw how they made them in Denver.

"Where is the paraffin?" he asked his new boss. "That is what makes them chewy."

"We use milk instead. We get chewy caramels without paraffin."

Milton watched as the man blended milk with sugar and vanilla. "But the candy will spoil too quickly."

"No, the cooking keeps it from spoiling. These can sit on the shelf for weeks."

Milton had to admit, the caramels were better than his. They were soft, smooth, and sweet. He watched the process carefully and memorized every step. This lesson alone was worth the trip to Denver.

After a few months, Milton was an expert at making milk caramels. He told his father, "No one has this recipe back East. I could be the first."

"You surely do not want to go back to Lancaster," Henry said.

"No. Nor Philadelphia, either. But I have had enough of Denver. The town is full of criminals. And, anyway, this city already has a source of milk caramels. Perhaps some other large city . . ."

"Chicago!" Henry said. "I have always wanted to go there."

Milton shrugged. Why not try Chicago?

They made candy in a Chicago basement. But after just a few months, Milton knew he hadn't found the right place for him. One evening he stared at his dinner of pork and beans, and then pushed it away. "Chicago is worse than Denver," he said. "The city is filthy, and people are miserable. What is the point of trying to produce a good product when no one cares?"

Henry leaned back in his chair. "Give it time. We must think big and expand."

"How can we?" Milton asked. "We have no money. We are barely paying our current bills."

"You could write to your aunt Mattie," Henry suggested.

Milton just shook his head. He knew his aunt would not fund any business if Henry was involved. Milton was beginning to think she was right. He loved his father, but Henry spent money faster than they could make it. If he had an extra dime, he spent it on food and drink in a beer garden.

"I can not stand Chicago any longer," Milton

said. "I am thinking of going home."

"Home!" Henry gasped. "You mean Lancaster? That cow town? Where your uncles live? What sane man would live in a place like that? Here, you could have all the wonders of the city."

"I have found very little here that is wonderful," Milton said. "And if there are ten honest men in this entire city of half a million, I have yet to meet them. No, I'm going back to Lancaster."

Henry frowned. Finally he said, "Do as you must. But I will not go back there to be nagged and criticized. I will stay here in Chicago. I may have a chance to work as a business agent for a fellow I met." He stared into the distance, his eyes misting over with dreams. "I can use the Palmer House hotel as my address. That will impress people."

Milton hid a smile. He had not told his father his whole plan. Yes, he would go back to Lancaster, but not to stay. He would ask his aunt to fund him in another business. Perhaps in New York City. Milton would never lie to his father, but this time he did not tell the whole truth. His only hope of getting his aunt's help was to leave Henry behind.

The Snavelys were doing well, and Mattie had money to spare. When she heard Milton's plan, and tasted his new caramel recipe, she gave him her blessing. "But are you sure about New York?" she asked.

"It is a large city with many rich people. But this time, I will not start a business in a city I do not know. I will find a job at some other candy store. I will learn as much as I can about the city and the competition."

He took a train to New York. The city of more than one million people had hundreds of candy stores. Most sold their products within their own neighborhoods. The rich bought the finest treats, while the poor took anything cheap.

Milton found a job at Huyler's Candies, a large business with two busy stores. The owner, Jacob Huyler, was pleased to get an employee with so much experience. Milton worked hard, while trying to learn everything he could about business in New York.

"How do you succeed with so much competition?" he asked one day.

"Location is the key," Mr. Huyler said. "Here on Broadway, rich women flock to Ladies' Mile to buy their fashionable clothes. We are handy when they want a break for refreshments. The store in the financial district gets the businessmen. They love little luxuries, and will buy expensive candies for their wives or sweethearts."

Milton nodded. Selling to the rich was a good way to make money. Yet his heart lay with the poor, especially the children. Didn't they deserve treats too? Milton remembered how much a simple lemon drop meant to him as a child.

In his spare time, Milton wandered the streets of the city. He found neighborhoods with huge mansions. The people going in and out wore expensive clothes. They even dressed their babies in diamonds. These people bought expensive luxury goods. They shopped in the large new department stores, where the clerks acted like servants.

Other neighborhoods were populated by poor working people. They bought cheap, mass-produced goods at neighborhood stores. Canned foods were becoming popular. Some manufacturers had found a much better way than Henry's disaster with the tomatoes.

The poorest of the poor lived wherever they could. Some built illegal shacks around Central Park, at the edge of the city. They were often lucky to eat at all.

Milton worked for Mr. Huyler during the day. In the evenings, he made caramels and sold them in the streets. He saved his money, and looked for a good place to start his business.

Milton found a little store on Sixth Avenue between Forty-second and Forty-third streets. The neighborhood was growing quickly, as the city expanded. New businesses opened nearly every day. A wide range of social classes lived close together. Rich people owned nice houses, while the middle class and poor rented apartments. The Colored School No. 3 was just one block to the south. Milton liked the mix of people.

Early in 1884, Milton opened his store. Soon he was making and selling candies seven days a week. His mother and aunt moved up from Lancaster to help him. They wrapped the candies and put them in boxes.

"Such a city!" Fanny exclaimed. She had to raise her voice over the rumble of the elevated train. "Ash and cinders raining through the air from those monsters, and all that noise." She smiled at Milton fondly. "But I suppose you enjoy living right under these newfangled contraptions."

"The noise and the dirt bring something good with them," Milton said. "Customers! Every weekend people take that elevated train here to the Croton Reservoir. Young couples love to walk along the wide walkways on top of the walls. Families play in the park. All that exercise makes them hungry." He grinned at his mother and aunt. "And then they come to us."

"Milton has become a good businessman," his aunt said. Her quick fingers didn't pause as she spoke. The pile of wrapped caramels grew. "But Milton, what about chocolates? The big stores do a good business with them."

"They are not worth the trouble. They are so hard to make, and too expensive for most of our customers." Milton peered into a copper kettle. The candy was not yet ready, so he kept stirring. "Everyone is trying to copy the Swiss. They have found a way to make smooth chocolate. But no one knows their secret. Here we can only make brittle, grainy chocolate."

"I suppose you are right," Fanny said.

152

"Everyone can afford hard candies and caramels."

"Well, perhaps not everyone," Milton said.
He remembered the poor children, dressed in
rags, in the city's worst neighborhoods. Many
were orphaned or abandoned. They lived on
the streets and hunted for food in the garbage
piles. He had tried to keep his mother and
aunt away from those areas.

But Aunt Mattie said, "I know what you
mean. Someone left a newspaper on the table
the other day. It had terrible photographs of
children working in factories. I gather that the
slums here are full of crime and disease."

"How can people be so cruel?" Fanny said.

Milton pulled the kettle off the stove and
poured it out before speaking again. "It is hard
to imagine how people can treat children that
way. I wish I could help."

"At least your work makes people happy,"
Fanny said.

"Yes," Milton said. "But I would like to do

more. If I make enough money, I would like to help some of those children." He had been poor as a child, and sometimes cold and hungry. But he had been loved. He felt lucky compared to what he saw in the big city.

"Your sales are growing by the week," Mattie said. "You will be well off soon."

Milton grinned. "A real success at last? That would be nice."

But a few months later, Henry Hershey showed up at the door.

No Help

Two years. This time, the shop only lasted two years.

As he locked the shop doors for the last time, Milton thought, *You would think I'd be used to failure by now. But it is just as painful every time.*

How could he have been such a fool? Once again, he had been swept up in Henry's dreams. Milton had wanted so badly to believe. He wanted the success for his father even more than for himself. But everything had gone wrong.

Milton spent a lot of money for equipment to make cough drops with his father. But the Hersheys could not compete with more popular brands. Henry left the business first. He even sold cough drops on his own, in another part of the city.

Henry stayed in New York while Fanny and Aunt Mattie had already gone back to Lancaster. Soon Milton would follow them. The candy-making equipment was on its way there as well. He had even boxed up the last of the sugar and molasses. It would be waiting for him. He just had to find a way to pay the shipping costs. Otherwise, the stationmaster would hold on to the crates.

Milton headed to the train station. He had enough money for his ticket home, and not a penny more. As he walked through the filthy streets of New York, Milton thought, *Perhaps I am a country boy after all. I do not seem to have what it takes to survive in the big city. I don't think I will even miss it.*

· · ·

A few days later, Milton walked the five miles from Lancaster to the big Snavely house. He was sweating in the summer heat, but the long walk had given him time to think. He paused, removed his hat, and mopped his brow. It wouldn't be easy to ask his uncles for more help. But what choice did he have?

Milton had been carrying his coat over his arm for the last few miles. Now he put it back on and straightened his cravat. He could at least look like a gentleman, even if his pockets were empty.

He went up the steps and rapped on the door. He took off his hat while he waited.

The door swung open. His uncle Benjamin stood there.

Milton cleared his throat. "I would like to speak to you and Uncle Abraham."

Benjamin nodded. "Come into the parlor, I will get my brother." He led the way to the formal parlor, which was used for business.

Milton sat on one of the stiff-backed armchairs. Dark wallpaper and heavy curtains made the room dim and close. No decorations adorned the walls or fireplace mantel. The room represented wealth without luxury.

Abraham entered, with Benjamin behind him, and greeted Milton solemnly. Milton looked at their stern faces and swallowed hard. Asking these proud, tough men for help was worse than facing any banker. But Milton had already been to every bank in Lancaster. No one would give him a loan, with his poor credit.

His uncles sat side by side on the sofa. Milton knew they did not care about wasting time on pleasantries. He cleared his throat and got straight to business. "I know you must be disappointed in the failure of the New York store. We all are. But I have learned a great deal from that experience."

"And from Philadelphia?" Abraham asked.

Milton flushed. "Yes. I know my record

is not good. But I think I know how to do better. It was a mistake going to a big city. I was an unknown among hundreds of competitors. But in Lancaster, people know me, and they know the Snavely name. It will be easier to make connections, and build trust."

"I don't know about that," Abraham said. "They know the Hershey name as well."

Milton clenched his jaw. He could not get into an argument about his father. He took a deep breath and went on, as if Abraham hadn't spoken. "I have a wonderful caramel recipe, from Denver. No one here has anything like it. Word will spread around Lancaster quickly. I can use local milk, which will be healthy and less expensive. In New York City it costs dearly to import the milk."

His uncles gazed at him without expression.

"I already have most of the equipment I need," Milton said. "I have arranged to rent a small room in a warehouse. I even have some of the ingredients. But I need money to rent a store, and to pay off my debts." He paused to clear his throat. It was hard forcing the words out. They seemed to echo around that silent room.

"I know I have no right to ask you for another favor. But the banks will not give me credit. If you give me another chance. . . ." He trailed off. What could he promise? To work hard? He had done that in Philadelphia and New York City. He had earned nothing but debt. He could not guarantee success this time either. He could only try.

Abraham and Benjamin exchanged a look. With a sinking heart, Milton realized that they had made their decision before he arrived.

"I am sorry," Abraham said. "We have taken enough chances on you. We have decided that you are not a good investment."

Milton tried to keep his face calm.

"I'm afraid there is too much of your father in you," Abraham said. "It is a shame. But you cannot expect us to spend our whole lives making up for our sister's foolish husband."

Milton stared at him. He got up and made a small bow. "Very well. I am sorry to have bothered you."

He walked from the room without looking back, and let himself out of the house. He paused in the shade of the porch and took a deep breath. He was trembling.

So that was it. The Snavelys had given up on him. He was a Hershey, and to them, that meant failure. He would not ask them for help again.

With the big, quiet house at his back, Milton looked down the road toward Lancaster. The farm fields seemed to shimmer in the heat. When he stepped off the porch, he would be walking away from the Snavely lifestyle. Sober, hard work, with a focus on profit rather than people. Stern moral standards. A home full of comforts, but no laughter.

Ahead lay the unknown. Milton was on his

own, for the first time in his life. He wouldn't have his mother pushing him one way, and his father dragging him the other. He wouldn't have his aunt's money and good sense to fall back on. He had only himself.

And yet, a weight seemed to lift. Whatever happened next, Milton would succeed or fail on his own terms. He would have no one else to blame or thank. He was twenty-eight, and becoming a man at last.

Milton smiled, stepped into the sunshine, and headed back to Lancaster.

Starting Over

A few days later, Milton finished his first batch of Denver-style caramels. He didn't have a shop, so he would sell them in the streets, from a handbasket. Perhaps it was better that way. He could go to people, instead of waiting for them to come to him.

He put a caramel in his mouth and chewed slowly. The rich, buttery taste melted over his tongue. Yes, he believed in this product. Using milk instead of paraffin made all the difference. It made the treat healthier, too. Twenty years ago, no one would have believed that. Milk spoiled too quickly, and could be dangerous even to drink. But now pasteurization was making milk safe. People saw it as wholesome.

Milton wrapped up his caramels, remembering how his mother and aunt had done that job so many times. He missed their company, but at the same time, it was good to be on his own. Working alone gave him time to think and plan. He made his own decisions, without anyone else's influence. He felt more in charge now than when he had owned a large business.

Milton piled caramels into the basket, lifted it, and went outside. He walked through the streets of Lancaster. He greeted people he had not seen in years. Many agreed to buy a few caramels, just as a kindness. Milton knew that once they had tried them, they would want more.

He went into a general store and gave the

owner a free sample. The man thanked him briefly and put it aside for later. Milton gave him a confident smile. "I'll check back tomorrow, and take your order."

The man chuckled, but he looked at the caramel with new interest. He was unwrapping it as Milton glanced back from the door.

By the end of the day, Milton had emptied his basket. He had made a few dollars. More importantly, he had made a start.

A few months later, Milton answered a knock at the door. "Mother! Aunt Mattie!" He greeted them with kisses and ushered them inside. "It is wonderful to see you."

Fanny gave him a shy smile. Mattie said briskly, "We have come to see your business."

Milton laughed. "That won't take long." He had moved into a larger space in a red-brick factory, but still worked alone. He showed them around the room. "I can't use the big equipment. I don't have the space, or

166

the money for ingredients. I am focusing on caramels just now. I have been experimenting with adding more milk. I have several orders from shopkeepers around town."

"We know," Mattie said. "We have been hearing about you." She looked around the room with her hands on hips. "Yes, you have been doing well on your own. Now we are here to help."

Milton grinned. "You have forgiven me?"

Mattie blushed. "It is not a matter of forgiveness. You had to prove you could stand on your own, and not give up."

"It was hard staying away," Fanny said. "But Mattie convinced me that you needed time to be a man, on your own."

"And I'm not offering you money, just our work." Mattie looked him in the eye and frowned. "But you must promise me one thing: If your father comes back, you must turn him away."

Milton thought for a minute. Finally he

said, "I cannot promise to turn him away from my door. But I promise I will not make him a partner, or take his business advice ever again. If I have not learned that lesson yet, then I'm too big a fool to deserve success."

Mattie smiled. "Very well. That will do."

Fanny hugged Milton. "I am so glad. I have not known what to do with myself lately." She looked at the big copper kettle on the stove. "You had better get busy with the next batch. We will start wrapping."

Milton came in after a long day's work. Fanny and Mattie had another batch of caramels wrapped in tissue paper, ready for the next day. Milton took off his hat and coat and sat down with a sigh. "I did good business today. The pushcart lets me go farther. But it is tiring, making caramels, and then spending the rest of the day selling them."

Fanny brought him some supper. "You could expand business if you had more employees."

Milton nodded. "And more equipment. I wish I had time to experiment, too. But it is hard to save up money for more employees or new equipment. All the money has to go back into supplies."

"Perhaps you should visit the banks again," Fanny said.

Milton shook his head. "Nothing has changed since last month. They will not take a chance on me." He glanced at his aunt, but knew he could not ask her for more money. He ate supper, quiet and thoughtful. Milton felt torn. He did not want to take another big chance, and perhaps lose all his money again. And yet, he had a popular product. Should he just keep the business as it was? Forever working from a warehouse, and selling caramels from a pushcart?

They were happy enough now, but they worked hard for little money. Milton still dreamed of buying a big house for them all. His mother and aunt were getting older. They might not always want to spend their days wrapping caramels. Someday, perhaps, he'd like to marry and have a family. He didn't have much to offer a wife now. To make more money, he had to enlarge his business. But did he dare to take that chance?

Milton pondered all through dinner. Finally he made his decision. He gazed across at his aunt and mother. "I believe it is time to expand. It is the only way to get ahead. I do not want to make the mistakes I've made before. But everything is in place. This is the time to take a risk."

"It is your decision," his mother said. "I will stand by you in whatever you think is best."

Mattie frowned and tapped the table. "It is risky, but you may be right. We cannot go on like this forever. But how will you do it?"

Milton took a deep breath. "The banks will not loan me any more money. I am not asking you for money, but could you lend your name to a loan? Then the banks might take a chance on me."

Mattie gave him a long look. "I must think about it."

In the morning, Milton made another batch of caramels and left them to cool. Then he took the candy from yesterday and loaded it into his pushcart. All day he wondered about Mattie as he smiled and chatted with his customers. Would she take another chance on him, or had he disappointed her too many times?

When he got back to the shop, he tried to act like it was an ordinary day. He didn't want to push Mattie in her decision. But his hands shook as he hung up his hat, and he stuttered his greeting.

"Come sit down," Mattie said.

Milton sat across from her and gazed into her stern face.

"I have made a decision," Mattie said. "I have a small row house on South Queen Street. I will put that up as collateral against your loan."

172

Milton jumped up and kissed his aunt's cheek. "Thank you!"

She held up a hand. "It is not much, and they will probably not give you a large loan. But you must do the best you can with it."

"I will. I will not disappoint you again."

Milton got a loan for seven hundred dollars. That was enough to buy some new equipment, including a big copper boiling pot. But Milton had only ninety days to pay back the loan. He rushed to make as many caramels as he could. But where would he sell them? With only thirty thousand people in Lancaster, the market was limited. Milton had to get his caramels to a bigger market.

I just need a little luck, Milton thought. *With all my hard work, it will be luck that makes or breaks me.*

Weeks passed. Milton worked long hours making and selling candy. He was making more money, but wasn't sure if he could pay the loan on time. He had already visited nearly every shop in Lancaster that might buy candy. Most had placed orders for his caramels. But would it be enough? He only had a few days left.

Someone rapped on the door. Milton opened it and saw a slender man, elegantly dressed. "Good morning," he said with a British accent. "Are you Mr. Hershey?"

Milton invited him in. "What can I do for you?"

The man studied the candy kitchen. He nodded to Fanny and Mattie, who kept quietly wrapping caramels. "My name is Decies. I am an importer from England, and I'm always looking for new products. I tasted some of your caramels in a store here in town." He smiled at Milton. "I believe I could sell your caramels in England. I would like to test it out. I will place a large order. If you can fill it in a timely manner, and if the caramels survive the sea journey in good form, then perhaps we can set up regular orders."

Milton stared at the stranger. His candies, selling halfway around the world? It was hard to imagine!

"Do you think you can do it?" Mr. Decies asked. Again he glanced around the kitchen. "It must be a large order to make it worth the trouble, tens of thousands of caramels. The candies will spend about a week on the ship. Then we must get them into the stores, and they must last long enough to be good for the customers. Is it possible?"

"Oh, yes!" Milton said. "We can do that."

The two men discussed the terms. By the time the Englishman left, Milton could hardly catch his breath. He stared at his mother and aunt. "This is it. This is the break I need."

Fanny rushed over to hug him. "But can we do it?" Mattie asked. "We will have to double production. And will the caramels last long enough?

"I'm not sure," Milton admitted. "They last

for several weeks, but I don't know what the trip at sea will do to them. This will be hard. We don't have much time to get the order ready. We will need more money for equipment and employees, and the shipping costs. He won't pay anything until the order arrives in good condition."

"What will you do?" Fanny asked.

Milton took a deep breath and let it out slowly. "I must go back to the bank. Perhaps they will give me more time on the loan, and advance some more money."

He hurried to the bank. He got in to see a junior officer named Frank Brenneman. Milton explained the situation.

Mr. Brenneman frowned. "It is too much of a risk for this bank."

"Please," Milton said, "just come and see my operation. See what we do, and then make your decision."

Mr. Brenneman gazed at Milton. Finally he sighed. "All right, I will come and take a look.

176

But do not get your hopes up. I'm sure the bank would not approve such a large loan."

They went back to the factory, and Milton showed Mr. Brenneman around and had him taste the caramels. Milton had to raise his voice above the racket from the wagon maker next door. Dirt filtered in through the windows.

"I know we are small," Milton said, "but we have done good business so far. This order could be the start of something huge. I just need a chance."

Mr. Brenneman looked around. "Give me a day to think about it."

When he left, Fanny said, "He did not seem impressed."

"Are you sure it was wise to bring him here?" Mattie asked. "Will he really want to give a loan to a young man and two old ladies?"

Milton shrugged. "I did not know what else to do. I could not lie to him, or pretend that we are more than we are. Tomorrow we will see."

Taking Chances

When Milton entered the bank the next morning he found Frank Brenneman pacing the floor. The men sat down and stared at each other. Milton could not think of anything to say, so he just waited.

"The bank will never approve this loan," Mr. Brenneman said at last. "They do not take chances like this."

Milton swallowed hard and tried to hide his disappointment.

"But I am willing to take a chance," Mr.

Brenneman said. "You were honest with me. You didn't hide how tough things are for you, or make excuses for it. I believe you are a risk worth taking."

At first Milton couldn't comprehend what Mr. Brenneman had said. "Then you mean . . . but, how? If the bank . . ."

Mr. Brenneman smiled. "I will sign my own name to a note for one thousand dollars. That way, we will avoid questions from the senior officers. I am taking a great chance on you, Mr. Hershey. Do not fail me."

Milton stood up and offered his hand. "You can count on me."

The next few weeks were a bustle of activity. Milton barely slept. He had to install the new equipment, and hire people to help. They made caramels day and night. When the caramels had been cooled and cut to size, Fanny and Mattie wrapped each individually in tissue paper. At last they had the order packaged and ready to ship.

After the caramels shipped, all Milton could do was wait. Would the caramels survive the long trip at sea? Would they arrive in time? Would the British importer pay, even if the caramels were good? They had only his promise.

"Mr. Brenneman at the bank has taken a chance on me," Milton said. "We must take a chance as well and trust Mr. Decies. It is out of our hands now." He took off his apron, put on his hat and coat, and went out with his pushcart to sell caramels around Lancaster.

Two more weeks passed. They knew it would take one week for the caramels to get to England. It would take another week for the check to get back, if everything went well. The loan was due in just a few days. Would they make it in time? Or would this be another expensive failure? Milton couldn't bear to let people down again.

Finally a letter came. Milton opened it, let out a whoop, and danced around. Fanny and

Mattie hurried over. "What? What is it?"

"A bank draft from England. For five hundred English pounds—that's over two thousand dollars!" Tears sprang to Milton's eyes. He said with a choked voice, "This will cover all of our debt."

Mattie and Fanny laughed and hugged him. "Good work, son," Fanny said.

Mattie put a hand to her chest. "It is quite a relief! I must admit, I have been worried. But you came through."

"Our worries are over," Milton said. "Mr. Decies wants to make large regular orders. I am going to the bank at once."

He grabbed his coat and ran out. Halfway down the block, he realized he still had on his caramel-splattered apron. He laughed and tucked up the apron. It would not show under his coat.

He hurried into the bank and held out the English check to Mr. Brenneman. "I am ready to pay off my loan."

• • •

From that point, the company grew and grew. Milton looked back on those early years with amazement. Who would believe that the rich and successful owner of the Lancaster Carmel Company had started in poverty? Who would believe he had failed so many times, before finally finding success? Who would believe that the Hershey name was once associated with foolish dreams and failure? Now it meant quality and success.

After five years building his business, Milton gazed upon his factory with pride. He had taken over the entire redbrick building, and had seven hundred employees. Once again, he had hired Harry Lebkicher to help manage the accounts.

Milton finally had time to experiment with new candy. His company offered caramels in many sizes, shapes, and prices. He added nuts to some, and he covered others with sugar icing. He experimented with corn syrup, a new sweetener that gave caramels a better chew. Hershey's Crystal A caramels, made with fresh milk, promised to "melt in your mouth." Premium lines such as Cocoanut Ices attracted the rich, while the poor could get other candy cheap, some were eight for a penny.

Milton opened another factory in Chicago, to serve the Midwest. Then he needed two more factories in Pennsylvania. They all operated twenty-four hours each day. The Lancaster Carmel Company grew to 1,400 employees. Milton's caramels sold across the country, and even as far away as Australia and Japan.

"Well, Milton," Fanny said, "your success is enough now even for my brothers. You are the number-one caramel manufacturer in the country. You have made it!"

Milton nodded. His dreams had come true. He owned a fine house in Lancaster. He ate the best foods. He had traveled the world, leaving the factory in Harry Lebkicher's capable hands. He had filled his house with treasures from his travels: paintings from Egypt and Mexico, sculptures from Italy, and stuffed tropical birds.

"But now what?" Milton asked. "I have more money than I know what to do with. I do not enjoy the business part of the business—accounting, distribution, sales. I only enjoy making candy."

"You came up with a new recipe just last week."

"Yes, that was fun. But I cannot be in the factory every day, getting in the way. I must let the employees do their work." Milton thought for a while. "Perhaps I will visit the Columbia Exposition. I can stop by the Chicago plant while I'm out there." Milton smiled. "At least, that will be my excuse. I really just want to see all the new inventions at the fair. Who knows? Maybe I will find something we can use here. I am ready for a change."

Chocolate Is the Future

Milton enjoyed many of the fair's delights. He watched Buffalo Bill's Wild West Show. He admired New York Central Railroad's Engine Number 999, which could travel at a record speed of 112 miles per hour. He rode on a new amusement, the Ferris wheel. He saw the greatest inventions of 1893.

One day, Milton strolled through the Agriculture Hall. It displayed foods from around the world: barrels of grain, stacks of smoked meats, canned goods, and more. Then Milton stopped and stared. A little temple rose thirty-eight feet high in front of him. The foundation was made of shining dark brown blocks. Columns with swirls of white and brown supported a dome. The building would have been impressive if it were made of stone. But Milton could see at a glance that it was not.

The temple was built entirely of chocolate.

Milton eagerly read the information on a sign on the wall. The Stollwerck brothers of Cologne, Germany, had made the masterpiece. The foundation blocks were dark chocolate. The columns included swirls of white cocoa butter. Milton stepped inside and stared up at a larger-than-life statue. The statue stood on a pedestal and held a sword—all made from chocolate.

"You could not do that with caramel." He laughed.

Later he visited the Machinery Building and saw something even more amazing. A German company had set up a full-size chocolate factory.

Milton studied the entire process with

delight. Ovens roasted the cocoa beans. After they cooled, they were hulled and ground. Then they went to special mixers. Marble rollers crushed them into a smooth chocolate paste. Presses squeezed moisture out of the paste. Another machine added sugar, vanilla, and cocoa butter. The result looked like a silky mud. It went into square molds, where it cooled. Finally, chocolate bars came out.

Milton inhaled deeply. Other exhibits smelled of grease and oil. The chocolate factory smelled rich and sweet. Milton knew the smell from the days when he had used chocolate to coat other candies. But it had never filled the air or flooded his senses this way.

The man showing off the display, J. M. Lehmann, offered Milton a chocolate bar. "The Europeans devour chocolate," the man hollered over the noise of the machines. "With mass production, the price is low enough for the average person."

Milton bit into the chocolate and let the

flavor wash over his tongue. "This is better than anything I have had in America. It is so smooth and rich!"

Mr. Lehmann nodded. "Americans do not know how to make a smooth chocolate."

"You can really make this at a price that everyone can afford?"

"Oh, yes. Chocolate is the future. Experts say factory workers should snack on chocolate so they can keep working hard. Some places are feeding chocolate to orphans, to keep them strong. Temperance groups tell people to eat chocolate instead of drink alcohol."

Milton nodded. From his travels in Europe, Milton knew that chocolate was growing popular there. In Britain, Quaker families owned many of the chocolate businesses. Like Mennonites, the Quakers believed in simple living and a strong community. They saw chocolate as part of a wholesome lifestyle.

Milton spent the rest of the afternoon asking questions about the chocolate equipment.

By the time he left, his mind was buzzing.

Over the next few weeks, Milton kept returning to the Machinery Building, and the chocolate factory. In the end, he made a decision. "The caramel business is a fad. But chocolate is something we will always have. It is a food as well as a candy." When he was ready to leave Chicago, he went to the chocolate display. "I want to buy your factory."

Lehmann smiled. "We will have machines shipped from Germany at once."

"I don't want new machines," Milton said. I want *these* machines. I know how they work. I know everything about them. As soon as the fair ends, I want you to send this entire factory to Lancaster."

An engineer set up the equipment in Lancaster. A few months later, Milton's company was making chocolate.

At first, they focused on baking chocolate, cocoa powder for drinking, and chocolate coatings for caramel. But Milton spent entire days experimenting. He also hired experts from other chocolate makers around the world. Together they came up with dozens of new candies.

Eventually they would produce more than one hundred types of "vanilla sweet chocolate" candies, which would later be called semisweet or dark chocolate. Hershey made chocolate dominoes, Easter eggs, and other novelties, besides more common candies like chocolate wafers.

Milton often returned to the house he shared with his mother, whistling cheerful tunes.

"It is good to see you enjoying your work again," Fanny said as he stepped on to the porch.

Milton smiled and took a seat next to her. "So long as I can experiment, I am happy." He turned sober. "I'm only sorry Aunt Mattie could not be here to see all of this." His aunt had died of pneumonia a few months after Milton bought the chocolate machinery, in April of 1894.

"You were like a son to her," Fanny said. "You made her very proud."

"I am glad of that." Milton hesitated, then plunged ahead. "But Mother, I have been thinking about Father. Who knows what he's doing in Colorado?"

Fanny snorted. "Spending your money and getting into trouble, no doubt."

"He is sixty-four years old," Milton said. "Too old to be wandering about. I would like to bring him home."

"Do not expect me to welcome him, or to share a home with him."

"Why must you pretend that you are a widow?" Milton asked. Fanny had listed herself as a widow in a Lancaster directory.

"I cannot divorce him, but I will not be married to him either. I wasted enough years on that man."

Milton sighed. "Very well. I will find another place for him to live." He began to smile. "Perhaps I will try to reclaim the

Hershey homestead. I can certainly afford to do that now."

"Your father will simply ruin the place again," Fanny said.

"He will not have the chance. I will hire a manager to take care of the place, and him." He gazed at his mother. "I want you to know that you can stop working anytime you wish. I know you are not interested in luxury. But you could spend your remaining years relaxing, visiting friends, or doing whatever you like."

Fanny gave his arm a squeeze. "You are a good son. But I am already doing exactly what I like. Wrapping candy keeps my hands busy. I only hope you will not find a machine to replace me. I will work until the day I die."

"Then I hope you will be wrapping candy for many years," Milton said. "No machine could ever replace you."

Fanny put her hands on her hips and gave Milton a stern look. "There's something else I want to say to you. You are a good son, and you would be a good father. You will be forty years old soon. Don't you think it is time to settle down?"

Milton frowned. "I always imagined myself marrying someday, and raising children. But for so many years I was too busy, and couldn't support a family. Now I have all the time and money I could want. But I cannot find a wife."

"You could have any available woman in Lancaster."

"I don't want any of the women in Lancaster. I feel they are interested in me because of my money."

Fanny nodded. "You must be careful about people like that. But surely, in all your travels, you could find someone suitable. A quiet, hardworking young lady with simple tastes."

Milton chuckled. He was not sure he shared his mother's ideas about a perfect wife. But he said, "I will keep my eyes open. One does sometimes find the most remarkable things on the road."

Kitty

Milton walked into A. D. Works, a popular confectionery shop and soda fountain in Jamestown, New York. Young men and women chatted at the tables. This was one of Milton's favorite stops when he went on sales trips. Many soda fountains were gathering places for young people. A. D. Works had something special. It reminded Milton of the busy energy at Royer's Ice Cream Parlor and Garden, when he was a boy.

He walked up to the counter. A young

woman turned and smiled at him. "Good morning. May I help you?"

Milton stared. The girl had a slim build and auburn hair pinned up on her head. She had wide gray eyes with thick lashes.

Finally Milton found his voice. "Good morning!" He glanced into the display case and pointed randomly. "I would like, um, one of those."

After she served him, Milton lingered, trying to think of something to say. This lovely girl would not be interested in him. She was much taller than Milton, and about twenty-five. He was forty, with gray starting to touch his hair and mustache. Yet he could not pull himself away.

She gave him another smile. "I have not seen you here before. Are you just passing through Jamestown?"

"I am here on business," Milton said. "It has been a few months since my last visit. You must be new since then."

"Yes, I have not been here long." She paused to serve another customer, but then turned back to Milton. "I hope you'll visit us again while you are in town. My name is Cathrine Sweeney, but my friends call me Kitty."

"I hope we will be friends," Milton said, "and that you will call me Milton." He felt himself blushing. "I know it is very forward of me."

Kitty laughed. "Life is too short to worry about the conventions." She held out her hand. "I am pleased to make your acquaintance, Milton."

Milton visited Jamestown as often as he could. A few months later, Kitty moved to New York City to work at a department store. Milton often took the train up to see her. He took her to dinner and the theater. But he did not tell anyone in Lancaster about her.

About a year after they met, Milton got ready for another trip. When he came downstairs with his small suitcase, his mother complained, "Not off again? You haven't spent a Sunday at home in over a year!"

Milton smiled at her. "That will change soon. I'm going to be married in New York, and then I will spend every Sunday at home."

Fanny gasped, and then began asking questions. Milton just chuckled. "You shall meet her soon enough." He left for New York, and his darling Kitty.

Kitty was Catholic, the daughter of Irish immigrants. She and Milton were married by a Roman Catholic priest at St. Patrick's Cathedral, on May 25, 1898. They did not invite any family members. This was a private ceremony, just for the two of them.

A few days later, Milton brought Kitty back to Lancaster. The news had made the local paper. Everyone wanted to see the new Mrs. Hershey. People stared and whispered as their carriage rolled down the street. By the time they pulled up in front of Milton's house, dozens of people had gathered. A few called out greetings to Milton. Others pretended they were just walking by. But it was obvious that everyone had come to see Kitty.

Fanny greeted them at the door. She looked Kitty up and down. "So you are the lady who has stolen my son's heart. I hope you will find our little town interesting enough for you."

Kitty gave Fanny a shy smile. "I hope we will become the best of friends."

"Of course." Fanny turned to watch as Kitty's trunks were carried into the house. "Goodness! Is all this yours?"

"I bought Kitty a large new wardrobe in New York," Milton said.

"I will help you unpack it," Fanny said. "Come, Kitty."

As they unpacked, Fanny studied each glamorous dress critically. Finally she turned to Kitty and asked, "Tell me, Kitty, have you ever been on the stage?"

Kitty heard the insult in the words. Actors and actresses were thought to have weak morals. Kitty smiled and said calmly, "I do love theater, but only as an observer. Now please excuse me. I wish to see my husband, and tour the rest of my house." She gently emphasized those last two words.

Kitty found Milton and told him what Fanny had said. "She doesn't like me! She resents me."

Milton held her. "She is used to being the only woman in my life. But I will not let her bully you. I will buy her another house, so this one will be ours."

As the months passed, Kitty settled in. "But your mother will never like me," she insisted.

Milton smiled. "My father does."

Kitty giggled. "He is a dear old man." Henry Hershey often visited, and got along with Kitty famously. That only annoyed Fanny more.

"The men admire you, and the children adore you," Milton said.

Kitty sighed. "But the women . . . I have made some friends. But I will never win over those old Mennonite women. It is bad enough that I'm Catholic. But it is worse that I cannot cook!" She threw up her hands and laughed.

"That's my Kitty," Milton said. "Just keep your sense of humor. I'll tell you what, let's go abroad again. We will get away from the gossip, and I will take a break from business."

Kitty shook her finger at him. "You can't fool me. You only go to Europe so you can find new ideas, and try new candies. You are never truly away from business."

"That is true," Milton admitted. He took Kitty's arms. "Here's what we shall do! I will sell the caramel company. I can't bear to give up the chocolate business, but my assistant can run it. Things go more smoothly when I'm not there, anyway. We can spend all of our time traveling."

● ● ●

Milton made a deal with the American Caramel Company in August, 1900. He received one million dollars for his caramel business. He kept the chocolate division. It introduced Hershey's Milk Chocolate in late 1900. The creamy, five-cent candy bar was quickly successful, and became the main Hershey product.

Two weeks later, Milton and Kitty boarded a boat for Europe. Kitty leaned against Milton as they gazed out at the ocean. "Just imagine, we can spend the rest of our lives on a world cruise," Kitty said. She turned her head to look at Milton. "But I wonder how long travel will keep your interest. I'm not sure you'll be happy without a business to build."

"I do not want another business," Milton said. "Business does not truly bring me happiness. But sometimes I wonder . . . The Cadburys in England have taken their factories out of the slums. They have built small, modern villages for their workers. They are making the world a better place."

"Your company provides jobs to hundreds of people," Kitty said. "You make a wonderful product that brings happiness to millions. *You* make the world a better place."

"But could I do more?" Milton asked. "We have one million dollars. We can't possibly spend that all on ourselves. Couldn't we do something good for others?"

"I knew it!" Kitty said. "There goes our vacation! You are already making plans for more work."

"Do you mind terribly?" Milton asked.

Kitty smiled. "No, I am only teasing. I would never ask you to give up your dreams. They make you who you are."

Making a Better World

Milton's travels only lasted a few weeks, but his plans for an ideal community took five years. People told him he was crazy, a foolish dreamer who could never succeed. But Milton had learned that some dreams were worth fighting for.

Milton scouted several areas, and finally settled on building his new factory town in the central Pennsylvania countryside. There he had a good water supply, fresh milk from the many dairy farmers, and easy access to railway lines for transportation. He could also find workers who had been raised to value honesty and hard work, as he had.

Milton built his new city at Derry Church, just a mile from where he was born. He hired a Lancaster engineer to draw up plans, but Milton helped with everything. He even chose names for the streets. The main roads through town were Cocoa and Chocolate Avenues. After all, profits from the Hershey Chocolate Company supported the town.

The new factory was one of the largest and most modern candy factories in the world. Limestone walls and slate roofs helped to prevent fires. The factory was seven hundred feet long, but just one story high so that workers wouldn't have to get down stairs during an emergency.

Milton wanted a lovely community that had everything the workers needed. To Milton, that didn't just mean basics such as public schools, churches, and the bank. He also planned parks, a public library, a swimming pool, a gymnasium, golf courses, and even a zoo. A trolley system carried people around town or to nearby towns.

Milton insisted that the houses all look different, not like cookie-cutter copies. They had modern conveniences like electricity, indoor plumbing, and central heating. Most people in America still had gas lights, outdoor water pumps, and outhouses. Workers and their families loved their new homes. The town had been expensive, but the happy workers felt loyal to the Hershey Company. Milton loved to ride the trolley through town and see all the smiles.

Those exciting years brought sad changes as well. Henry Hershey suffered a heart attack while walking through a snowstorm after visiting friends. He died a few hours later, on February 18, 1904. Fanny, who had called herself a widow for so many years, finally was one. She would live to be eighty-four, dying of pneumonia in 1920. She insisted upon being useful, and spent her days wrapping candies until the very end.

Finally Milton and Kitty could relax on the porch of their new home, a twenty-two-room white mansion called High Point. It looked out over the city Milton had built. It was hard to believe that such a bustling community had sprung up where only farm fields had been a few years before.

But when Milton gazed at his wife, he knew something was missing. He and Kitty were still in love. But Kitty suffered from a mysterious illness that often left her in pain. Sometimes she had a hard time controlling her body. She could not give Milton the family he'd wanted.

"You have that look again," Kitty said. "What are you thinking?"

"I am thinking about children," Milton admitted.

Kitty looked down at her hands. "I know how much you have wanted them, my love. I am so sorry—"

"You need never to apologize to me," Milton interrupted. He took her hand. "You are the best thing that ever happened to me. No, I have given up hoping for children of my own. But I can't stop thinking about all the children who do not have mothers and fathers. I'm thinking about an orphanage."

Kitty gave a little gasp. "You mean to build one? Oh, what a wonderful idea. Then we would have lots of children!"

Milton nodded. "I have long imagined building such a place, for orphaned boys. The biggest influence in a boy's life is what his dad does. When a boy doesn't have any sort of dad, his life is hard. Boys without a good family lack role models."

"Not if they have you as a father!" Kitty cried. "We will teach them to be honest and hardworking."

"We can make sure the younger children have plenty of exercise, and time to play. Older boys will get an education. But I think they should also get training in farming or a trade."

Kitty clasped her hands together. "Oh, Milton, can we really do it?"

"Of course we can!" Milton grinned. "What better way to spend our money? Money should be used for the good of the community, for the good of people. I don't want to die and leave a fortune for relatives to fight over. I would much rather have my money help children—now, and for generations in the future. Too many of these boys never get a chance. Well, I'm going to give some of them a chance my way!"

When Milton wanted a thing done, it happened quickly.

He welcomed the first boys to the school in 1910. Six-year-old Nelson Wagner and his little brother, Irvin, had recently lost their father. Their mother could no longer take care of them, and her nursing baby. When she got the letter admitting her boys to the Hershey Industrial School, she brought them with regret but also relief.

On a late summer's day, they walked up the big front porch of the Hershey Homestead, the school's first building. There they met fifty-three-year-old Milton Hershey, and the couple who would be their house parents. The boys shared a bedroom in the big old house. They would go to school in an old cow barn, do chores, and play in the fields and creeks.

Eight more boys came that fall. Soon, more than a hundred boys had a home at the Hershey Industrial School, which grew to include more group homes and classrooms. The school focused on clean living, hard work, and religious tolerance. Milton reviewed every application and helped to choose the boys. He visited them often at the school. Eventually, he would leave the school his entire fortune.

Once a year, Milton had all the boys to breakfast at High Point. Milton's hair and mustache were mostly gray now. Years of fine food had put extra weight on his thin frame. But in many ways he hadn't changed. He wore a simple gray suit, bowtie, and hat. His eyes still twinkled, and his shy smile put people at ease.

The boys used their best manners while they sat at the long tables set up on the lawn. They politely answered Milton's questions about their studies, and the work they did on the farms. Finally they had eaten the last piece of toast, and drained the last mug of cocoa.

Milton gazed from one young face to another. "Well, my boys, how shall we spend our Sunday afternoon? Perhaps you'd like to go back to your farms and catch up on chores?"

The boys squirmed, but said nothing.

Milton put a hand over his mouth and pretended to yawn. "Or it is a lovely afternoon for a nap. Perhaps you'd like to take naps?"

A few of the boys giggled. Two or three shook their heads.

"Well!" Milton said in mock exasperation. "You are hard to please. But wait, what's that I hear?" He cupped a hand to his ear. "Why, I believe it is music, down at the bandstand! I suppose," he said doubtfully, "we could go down to the park. That is, if you would rather visit the zoo and ride the carousel."

The boys cheered.

Milton grinned. "Very well. Push in your chairs and get in line. I will be with you in a moment."

Milton went onto the veranda, where Kitty sat. "I'm off with the boys, my darling," he said.

She held out her hand to him. "Oh, Milton, it is wonderful to see the boys so healthy and happy. I can see how grateful they are to you, for all you have done."

"I'm glad to do it. Of all my successes, this means the most to me."

"Because you can give others something you never had? I know you did not always have a happy childhood."

Milton grinned down at her. "I am having one now. That is enough."

For More Information

BOOKS

Aaseng, Nathan. *Business Builders in Sweets and Treats*. Minneapolis, MN: Oliver Press, 2005.

Brenner, Joël Glenn. *The Emperors of Chocolate: Inside the Secret World of Hershey and Mars*. New York: Random House, Inc., 1999.

Burford, Betty. *Chocolate by Hershey: A Story about Milton S. Hershey*. Minneapolis, MN: Carolrhoda Books, 1994.

Coe, Sophie D., and Michael D. Coe. *The True History of Chocolate*. New York: Thames & Hudson, 2007.

D'Antonio, Michael. *Hershey: Milton S. Hershey's Extraordinary Life of Wealth, Empire, and Utopian Dreams*. New York: Simon & Schuster, 2006.

Malone, Mary. *Milton Hershey, Chocolate King.*
Champaign, IL: Garrard Publishing Company,
1971.

VIDEOS

The Chocolate King: Milton S. Hershey. A&E Home
Video, 1995.

WEBSITES

Hershey Community Archives:
> hersheyarchives.org

Hershey Museum:
> hersheymuseum.org

Milton Hershey information:
> miltonhershey.com

Milton Hershey School:
> mhs-pa.org

★★★ Childhood of Famous Americans ★★★

One of the most popular series ever published for young Americans, these classics have been praised alike by parents, teachers, and librarians. With these lively, inspiring, fictionalized biographies—easily read by children of eight and up—today's youngster is swept right into history.

Abigail Adams
John Adams
Louisa May Alcott
Susan B. Anthony
Neil Armstrong
Arthur Ashe
Crispus Attucks
Clara Barton
Elizabeth Blackwell
Daniel Boone
Buffalo Bill
Ray Charles
Roberto Clemente
Crazy Horse
Davy Crockett
Joe Dimaggio
Walt Disney
Frederick Douglass
Amelia Earhart
Dale Earnhardt
Thomas Edison
Albert Einstein
Henry Ford
Ben Franklin
Lou Gehrig
Geronimo

Althea Gibson
John Glenn
Jim Henson
Milton Hershey
Harry Houdini
Langston Hughes
Andrew Jackson
Mahalia Jackson
Tom Jefferson
Helen Keller
John Fitzgerald Kennedy
Martin Luther King, Jr.
Robert E. Lee
Meriwether Lewis
Abraham Lincoln
Mary Todd Lincoln
Thurgood Marshall
John Muir
Annie Oakley
Jacqueline Kennedy Onassis
Jessie Owens
Rosa Parks
George S. Patton
Molly Pitcher
Pocahontas
Ronald Reagan

Christopher Reeve
Paul Revere
Jackie Robinson
Knute Rockne
Mr. Rogers
Eleanor Roosevelt
Franklin Delano Roosevelt
Teddy Roosevelt
Betsy Ross
Wilma Rudolph
Babe Ruth
Sacagawea
Sitting Bull
Dr. Seuss
Jim Thorpe
Harry S. Truman
Sojourner Truth
Harriet Tubman
Mark Twain
George Washington
Martha Washington
Laura Ingalls Wilder
Wilbur And Orville Wright

★★★ Collect them all! ★★★